His breath was warm against her cheek for the barest moment, and then his lips brushed over her temple, and her eyebrows, and her lashes, and finally, as she strained forward to meet him, they touched her lips.

She tasted brandy when he deepened the kiss, and an intoxicating flavor that belonged, she was sure, only to him. She was certain of nothing else, except a profound need to be closer still to the heat that radiated from his body. Mindlessly, she dissolved in his embrace and kissed him back.

And lost her heart. . . .

By Lynn Kerstan
Published by Fawcett Books:

FRANCESCA'S RAKE
A MIDNIGHT CLEAR

A
MIDNIGHT
CLEAR

Lynn Kerstan

FAWCETT CREST • NEW YORK

A Fawcett Crest Book
Published by Ballantine Books
Copyright © 1997 by Lynn Kerstan Horobetz

All rights reserved under International and Pan-American Copyright Conventions. Published in the United States by Ballantine Books, a division of Random House, Inc., New York, and simultaneously in Canada by Random House of Canada Limited, Toronto.

http://www.randomhouse.com

Library of Congress Catalog Card Number: 97-90215

ISBN 0-449-22770-7

Manufactured in the United States of America

First Edition: November 1997

10 9 8 7 6 5 4 3 2 1

For my beautiful goddaughters—Carly, Sidney, Kendall, and Maddie Hoshko—and for their wonderful parents, Margaret Ann and Michael. I love you all!

Prologue

When the parlor door opened, seven pairs of eyes gazed curiously at the white-faced woman who emerged, pressing a handkerchief to her brow.

"Oh," she mumbled. "Oh dear. Oh dear." She staggered across the entrance hall and out the main door.

The elderly lady who had introduced herself as Felicia turned to the remaining applicants, ensconced on wooden benches set against the walls. "Which of you is next?"

A stiff-backed, reed-thin woman stalked to the parlor door. "Miss Blimpstone," she announced imperiously.

Felicia scuttled ahead of her to make the introduction, and the door closed again.

My heavens, Jane Ryder thought, tugging her shabby portmanteau closer to her knees. Since her arrival, four other applicants had stumbled away in similar fashion. The mysterious employer must be a tyrant of the first order.

"What do you suppose is going on in there?" whispered the nervous young woman seated beside her. "I thought this was to be an interview for a secretarial position."

"Of course it is," Jane assured her. "Were you sent by the Farbes Agency, too?"

"I came from Simon and Sillaright. They have always placed me well before, but only in temporary positions. Not many employers will take on a female for more than a fortnight."

Jane nodded. She had yet to find a position for even so brief a period, and still owed Mrs. Tucker for a week's lodging. The widow had turned her out that very morning in favor of a boarder with ready cash.

She glanced at the women sitting on the bench across from her. All were staring fretfully at the parlor door, as if expecting it to burst into flames.

Jane rather wished that it would. A bit of fire and brimstone would send the others scampering, leaving the field to her. She'd been the last to arrive, after lugging all her worldly possessions for three miles in a sleet storm, and feared that another candidate would secure the job before it was her turn to be interviewed.

At this point she didn't care if it was Satan himself holding court inside that parlor. Better a warm night in hell than the one she faced on the icy streets.

She sat a little straighter on the hard bench, willing steel into her spine. Perhaps it had been a mistake coming to London, but there was no going back now. And surely she was overdue for a helping of good luck.

The Farbes Agency had not sent her out for a single interview since she registered with them a month ago. Nor did they have one for her today, until she bullied her way past the clerks and bearded Mr. Farbes in his office. A kindly, rather befuddled man, he apologized profusely for neglecting her.

"But, Miss Ryder, there are so few positions to be had in December," he had said. "With the gentry gone to their country estates for the holidays it is quite impossible to turn up anything appropriate. Could you come back in a few weeks, when Parliament is seated?"

"No I could not," she replied. And when she refused to be budged, demanding that he search his files for even the most inconsequential of openings, he reluctantly pulled a folder from his drawer and spread it open on the desk.

"In the normal course of things," he said, "I'd not wish to be involved with this matter. You may be sure I have sent no one to apply for the position. Disreputable business!" Shuddering, he dipped his pen in the ink pot. "But

2

if you insist, Miss Ryder, I shall give you the direction. For all I know, the position may have been filled long since, but this is all I have to offer at the moment."

Now she was here, and the position had obviously *not* been filled. Whatever that position was. She had rushed off before thinking to ask for details. *Impulsiveness has already got you in a great load of trouble,* she scolded herself. *One day it will be the death of you, my girl.*

The parlor door opened with a groan of metal hinges and Miss Blimpstone stomped out, her narrow cheeks clenching and unclenching as if she were sucking on a lemon. "Leave now if you know what's good for you," she advised contemptuously. "Spare yourselves the indignity I have just endured."

Two applicants, including the girl who had spoken to Jane, leapt to their feet and followed Miss Blimpstone. Jane crossed her fingers for luck. Only three to go, and then she would have her chance.

In the next half hour, Felicia called them in one by one. All emerged whiter than paper or blushing furiously. They shook their heads at Jane as they walked past, a silent warning to escape while she could.

She straightened her skirts, waiting eagerly to be summoned. *It's only the two of us now,* she told the mysterious figure behind the door. *Whatever it requires, I must find a way to make you keep me.*

Felicia beckoned then, inquired her name, and led her into a large, cluttered room lit only at the far end by two braces of candles and a flickering fire. Heavy tapestries lined the walls, and curtains of deep crimson velvet hung over the window. Jane wove among chairs, sofas, and claw-footed tables strewn with knickknacks, following Felicia on shaky legs.

Near the hearth was a small figure huddled in a Bath chair. Rather like a spider in its web, Jane thought, able to distinguish only a shape outlined by the flames behind it. A long-fingered hand with painted nails raised a lorgnette.

3

"Jane Ryder, is it?" The voice rang clear as a brass bell. "Not much of a name, Jane Ryder."

"No, ma'am. Were it left to me, I'd have chosen better."

She barked a laugh. "You're the one who brought her luggage, Felicia tells me. Planning to stay?"

"Only if I meet with your approval, ma'am. I trust you to tell me how I may do so."

"To begin with, do cease wringing your skirt. I ain't going to bite you. And come closer, where I can have a good look at your face."

Hands straight as sticks by her sides, Jane moved into the circle of light in front of the chair. The woman had arranged the candelabra so that she could see her victims while her own face remained in the shadows. Jane admired the tactic.

The woman peered through her lorgnette. "Ah. Plain as your name, I see. But just as well. I prefer to be the most beautiful woman in any room. Now tell me about yourself."

Jane cleared her throat, wondering what it was this exceedingly odd woman wished to hear. Her work experience, she supposed, and an accounting of her skills. She had acquired a great many in her four-and-twenty years, but few were the sort to be relevant in this place.

"I read and write in Latin and Greek," she began. "Also English, of course. I am used to taking dictation, have excellent penmanship, and my work habits are exemplary."

"Oh, *exemplary*, are they?" The woman chuckled. "Hoity-toity."

"I also possess an extensive vocabulary," Jane acknowledged, wishing her knees would cease knocking together.

"Useful. I wonder if you are acquainted with the specific words you will require for this project? But never mind that. It appears you lack the ability to answer a simple question. The subject at hand is *you*, gel. Who are you, where do you come from, and how came you to land in my parlor?"

Oh, Lord. How can it matter, you atrocious old biddy? Jane mustered a polite smile. "My life story is a tedious one, ma'am. If you don't mind, I prefer to keep it to myself."

"Well, I *do* mind," the woman shot back. "How am I to know you are not a burglar. Or an ax murderer?"

"Were I any such thing, I would hardly say so," Jane replied. "But if it reassures you, the constables are not on my trail, nor have they reason to be. I am simply a woman who must work to support herself, and I have come here in search of employment."

"And wondering what you got yourself into, I daresay. Oh, very well, missie. Since you refuse to give over at the moment, I'll answer a few of the questions you've been aching to ask me. Draw up a chair, Jane Ryder. Make yourself warm."

Jane pushed a heavy Egyptian-style chair across the thick carpet, lifted her worn brown cloak, and perched on the edge of the padded seat. For the first time, she was able to clearly see the woman's face.

Her skin was astonishingly white—coated with rice powder, Jane decided—and wrinkled like an elephant's hide. Her cheeks were garishly rouged, as were her lips, and long ruby earrings dangled from her earlobes all the way to her narrow shoulders. A helmet of lacquered ebony hair sat atop her head, two red ostrich feathers planted directly in the center.

Jane might have dismissed her as a dotty old eccentric, if not for the canny blue eyes that pronged her like a butterfly staked out on a blotter. Wise eyes, she knew immediately. Whoever she was, this woman was not to be trifled with.

"My name is Lady Eudora Swann," she said. "Ever heard of me?"

"I'm afraid not, ma'am. But I've only been in London

a few months." She couldn't resist adding, "Are you a famous ax murderer?"

"Not yet, you impertinent chit. Don't tempt me. Did the agency tell you nothing of me or this position?"

By now Jane was certain only that Lady Swann had no patience with milk-and-water misses. And a good thing, too, since Jane Ryder was nothing of the sort. If she got this job, please God, she would not have to pretend, as she often had, to be compliant and dim-witted. "Mr. Farbes said only two words to the point, ma'am. As I recall, they were *disreputable business*."

"Didn't keep you away, I see. But he was right. Or at the least, a great many people would agree with him. I care nothing for that. At five-and-eighty, I've long since learned to ignore the opinions of idiots and Methodists." She tugged her lap robe around her bony knees. "It is my intention, Miss Ryder, to compile a history of the English aristocracy."

"Good heavens! There are a great lot of aristocrats, ma'am."

"And most are dull as dust balls. I'll not waste a drop of ink on anyone it would bore me to talk about, so set your mind at ease. This will be a carefully selected history, from my own viewpoint, and I mean to concentrate on the scandals." She pulled out a lacy handkerchief and began polishing the glass on her lorgnette. "It will also be uncensored."

"Will someone publish this?" Jane asked. "Sell it in the bookshops?"

"Oh, indeed. But that is not the point. What I know— and I know a great deal—ought to be recorded. I expect to live another fifty years, but there will come a time when the stories I have to tell will die with me unless I write 'em down. And as I'm too lazy to do that, I want a secretary to listen to my tales and put them in order." She smiled. "People come to me every day for information, you know. They call me The Tongue. Since Farmer George took the throne, I have been the source of the most accurate information to be had. I've a retentive memory and have known everyone of importance for seventy years. The information must not be lost."

"Some information is better lost, ma'am. Most particularly the scandals."

Lady Swann's eyes narrowed. "If you believe that, young woman, this position will not suit you. Nor will you suit me."

"If you please, I fail to see why. I am perfectly able to take dictation on any subject, and the content of your book is wholly yours to select."

"I'll tell you why, Miss Sobersides. The book will never be completed if I fail to enjoy myself, and the last thing I need is a censorious secretary huffing as she scribbles and making sour faces at me when she thinks I'm not looking. But I am *always* looking. Nothing escapes me."

Jane could readily believe it. "What you *do* need, I apprehend, is someone capable of doing all the unpleasant parts, like the writing and editing, while you simply tell your stories. You may be sure I shall keep my thoughts to myself, Lady Swann."

"Which only means that I'll be wondering all the while what it is you are thinking, wretched gel. But let us put you to the test, shall we? You'll find writing materials on the secretaire. Seat yourself there and record every word I say."

Jane noticed a trash basket beside the small desk, overflowing with crumpled sheets of paper. The remains of previous dictations, she thought as she removed her gloves. Then she quickly checked the pen for sharpness, dipped it in the inkwell, and nodded to Lady Swann.

For the next five minutes, she wrote as fast as she could, abbreviating words in her self-devised shorthand and paying no attention whatever to their meaning. Lady Swann spoke in a steady flow, likely repeating the same story she had told several times that afternoon.

"Do you not heed me?" Lady Swann asked sharply.

Jane glanced at the last words she had inscribed. *That*

7

will do, Miss Ryder. "I beg your pardon, ma'am. I do not listen as I write, if you take my meaning."

"Ah." Lady Swann tapped her long fingernails on the arm of her chair. "That explains a great deal. Well, let's see if you got it right. Read back to me."

Jane lifted the first sheet of paper closer to the light and began to recount the exploits of the sixth Marquess of Fallon. Lord Fallon had a great many exploits to recount.

About halfway through, she glanced up at Lady Swann, who was regarding her with a curious expression.

"What think you?" she demanded. "Are you not offended? Horrified? So aquiver that the stays on your corset are rattling?"

Above all things, Jane wanted to laugh. But she was not at all sure how Lady Swann would react to that. "Am I meant to be shocked?" she inquired mildly. "His lordship is a depraved sort of fellow, and excessively vulgar, but thus far he has engaged in no activity more imaginative than what barnyard animals do as a matter of course."

Lady Swann's eyes crinkled with amusement. "Read on, m'dear."

"It's a-amazing," Jane managed to say when she was finished. Her eyes were beginning to water. "Perfectly dreadful, of course."

"But amusing?"

"Oh y-yes." She burst into laughter. "I'm sorry, Lady Swann. You must know that I don't understand the half of it. Nor can I begin to think why, let alone *how*, he did that business with the—but surely you are making this up?"

"Oh no. Believe me, even my imagination could not outpace what some people will come up with. That 'un's been dead these fifty years, but his father was just as bad and his son even worse. We'll have an entire chapter for the Marquesses of Fallon. Perhaps two or three."

We? Jane thought with a thrill of excitement. *Did that mean—?*

"You have the job," Lady Swann told her. "Assuming you still want it. I'll decide your salary later, when I determine what you are worth. You wish to move in immediately, I take it."

Jane slipped by habit into the demeanor expected of a servant. "If you please, ma'am."

"Very well. Felicia will show you to your room. We dine at eight o'clock, at which time you will begin to call me Eudora." She raised her lorgnette. "And I shall begin to discover exactly who and what you are, Jane Ryder."

Chapter 1

Lady Eudora Swann slouched in her Bath chair, chin buried in the folds of lace at her throat, her soft snore rumbling like the purr of a cat.

She slept more often during these long winter days, Jane had noticed. But here in this overheated parlor, its windows tightly sealed against the shrill December wind, her own eyes had a lamentable tendency to drift shut.

How easily a body got used to being warm and well fed. She had gained nearly two stone in the past year and had filled out enough above her waist to draw lingering glances from the gentlemen who came to call on Eudora.

But her time in this unique household would soon come to an end, she knew. Before the first spring crocus, *Scandalbroth* would be in the hands of the publisher, who fully expected the book to make him a wealthy man. Mr. Crumb paid frequent visits to check on its progress. Eudora's less controversial project, the *Swann History of Eighteenth-Century British Aristocracy*, was to be locked in the Bank of England and opened at the turn of the next century.

Jane rarely allowed herself to contemplate her departure and had made no plans for the future. Eudora paid her extremely well, and with few personal expenses, she had invested nearly all her salary and generous bonuses on the 'Change. For the first time in her life, she could confront the next stage of it without worrying about money for at least a year, perhaps two if she was frugal.

Rubbing the back of her neck, she studied the papers spread over the enormous desk Eudora had purchased for her use. Because Eudora did not like being alone, Jane did most of her work in the makeshift office created for her by the largest window, where she could look out over Upper Brook Street.

A militant banging at the door shot Eudora awake with a start. Moments later Felicia tottered into the room, followed by a tall, imposing gentleman wearing a caped greatcoat and high beaver hat. His sharp gaze swept the parlor, passing over Jane as if she were a footstool, and came to rest on Eudora.

"Lady Swann, I presume." He bowed curtly. "Pardon me for disregarding your"—he gestured in Felicia's direction—"footwoman. She informed me that you are not receiving, but this is a matter of some urgency."

Eudora waved a hand. "Company is always welcome, young man, so long as it minds its manners. Felicia, you may return to your nap."

The man stripped off his gloves, slapping them impatiently in the palm of one hand while waiting for Felicia to make her ponderous way to the door.

Jane wondered if she ought to take her leave, too, but Eudora said nothing, and it soon became apparent the man was unaware of her presence. Like a raptor shadowing prey, his attention was directed entirely at the tiny woman in the Bath chair.

"I am Fallon," he said. "Doubtless you have been expecting me."

"So I have," Eudora replied easily. "But you arrived in London all of nine weeks ago. What kept you?"

"None of your da—" He fisted his gloves in one hand. "I have been otherwise occupied, Lady Swann. It was only yesterday that I heard of your abominable book."

"Everyone's a critic," Eudora said with a dramatic sigh. "And like all the others carping at me, you have yet to read a word of it."

"I am here," he told her stonily, "to make certain that no one *ever* reads it. At the least, I insist you delete any and all references to my family."

"But I am writing an exposé of aristocratic scandals, sir. Should I excise the scurrilous doings of the Fallon clan from my book, only the merest pamphlet would remain." She clicked her tongue. "Do remove your hat, boy. With it on, you take up far too much space in this room."

So he did, Jane thought as Fallon tossed his curly-brimmed beaver onto a table. True, the wide greatcoat exaggerated the considerable width of his shoulders, but even stripped to the skin, this man would occupy more than his fair share of any room. It was less a matter of size than the assertive way he carried himself. He was in constant motion, claiming territory with his fingertips as they brushed along the back of a sofa or picked up a trinket and put it down again.

A restless man, she decided, and one who found it difficult to restrain his natural vitality. Now and again he paused, clearly willing his body into the pose of a disdainful aristocrat, but moments later he was on the prowl again.

Jane thought him fascinating. A man at war with himself, she suspected, watching as he forcibly stilled himself in front of Eudora's chair.

"Let us come to the point," he said irritably. "What will it cost me to buy the Fallons out of your book?"

"Buy?" Eudora snorted. "You imagine I am set on *blackmail*? Good Lord, I am six-and-eighty, young man. What's more, I was heir to my late husbands' fortunes—all six of 'em. What need have I for money?" She fluttered her kohl-blackened lashes. "On the other hand, you appear to be a remarkably healthy, energetic fellow, and well-looking in a rough-cut sort of way. Perhaps we can come to terms after all." She winked in Jane's direction. "What think you?"

He looked thoroughly bewildered.

"Well, you mull it over," Eudora said kindly. "But if there are to be negotiations, they will be conducted in my boudoir."

Jane pressed her hands over her mouth to keep from laughing aloud. The situation was all the more remarkable because Eudora's offer was quite serious. For a tumble with this virile young aristocrat, she would cheerfully consign the Fallon chapters to the fire.

When he finally twigged her meaning, his lordship was not amused. Stalking forward, he loomed over Eudora with clear menace. "I am, to my knowledge, the sole remaining Fallon, and it is therefore my duty to carry on the name. Such as it is," he added woodenly. "What my forebears have done should be permitted to rest in their graves with them, Lady Swann. Your book will make it impossible for me to restore the reputation they abandoned centuries ago."

"I expect that would be impossible in any case," Eudora advised him. "As it is, I reveal nothing in my book that is not generally known. Whatever the Fallon men did, they did openly. There was no scuttling about in dark corners, sinning in private and painting themselves virtuous in public. Well, I daresay they concealed a great many depravities, but nothing I have written about them has ever been a secret."

"To *you*, perhaps, and a few equally ghoulish vultures who feed on other people's lives. The scandals would be mostly forgot if you didn't put them up for sale in every bookstall from here to the Orkneys." His voice grew dangerously soft. "I had hoped you would be reasonable, Lady Swann. But if you persist with this reprehensible plan, I shall haul you into court on charges of slander and libel."

"Excellent!" Eudora rubbed her hands together. "More publicity for *Scandalbroth*. But you will need to prove malice on my part, and that will not be possible. For more years than you have been alive, boy, I have disseminated gossip with an even hand. I can summon scores, even hundreds, of witnesses to testify on my behalf. I am, in fact, a legend, while you are merely a Fallon. But sue away if you must. Should I live long enough for the courts to work their way through all the briefs and come to trial, you will unquestionably lose."

Jane knew instinctively that this man was unaccustomed to losing. She observed him closely, and when he raised his eyes to the window directly behind her, she was able to discern their uncommon color. Like clear dark amber, she thought, the irises rimmed with black. She saw, too, the anger that lit them from behind, as if a fire raged inside him.

"I see," he said to Eudora. "With this book, you crown your pernicious career as a scandalmonger. You indulge yourself with one last triumph before sliding into the grave."

"I might be offended," Eudora said with amusement, "if I gave a straw for your opinion. But as I do not, you may take your leave now. Unless . . ."

"Unless *what*!" Fallon visibly dug in his heels. "And no more rubbish about negotiations in a bedchamber."

"Do you know," she replied thoughtfully, "a smart man would be flattering me about now. But then, you are a true-bred Fallon, and no Fallon ever used his wits to advantage."

The marquess swept his hat from the table. "I am in residence at the Pulteney Hotel, Lady Swann. Contact me when you have a proposition of merit to offer. Otherwise, I'll see you in court."

From the door, obviously as an afterthought, he remembered to bow. Again Jane had the impression of a man resolved to do the proper thing, even when it went against his every inclination. And then he was gone, in a sweep of greatcoat and a clatter of boot heels against marble tiles in the entrance hall.

"Well!" Eudora exclaimed, looking ominously self-satisfied. "Who would have thought the Fallons capable of breeding such a promising young buck? Proud to his toenails, the new marquess. And handsome, although I expect he's been in more than one fight, what with that scar on his cheek and the off-kilter nose."

Jane hadn't noticed the scar or the broken nose, being more focused on a pair of oddly colored, beautiful eyes and his seething, barely contained energy. It had all but set the floorboards on fire. "Can he make trouble for you?" she asked.

"Oh, he can try. But I expect he'll soon realize that publicity from a lawsuit is the very last thing he wants. What will he try next, I wonder? It's certain he'll not give up so easily."

Jane began to sort the papers on her desk into piles. She had always thought publication of *Scandalbroth* a terrible idea, and sometimes felt that Eudora agreed. But enclosed in this house as she was, Eudora required excitement to keep her mind lively and her spirits high. While working on the book, she had revisited long-dead acquaintances and relived the pleasures of her youth.

All along, Jane had hoped she would settle for the achievement of writing the book and stop short of actually sending it to press. But she seemed determined to do so, if only because the scandal would draw more visitors to her door. Eudora thrived on company.

Jane suddenly remembered the hook Eudora had briefly dangled. "You never answered his lordship's question," she said. "Unless *what*?"

"Ah, yes." Eudora's eyes glittered. "Come sit here by me, my dear."

Jane added another log to the fire and pulled up a

15

chair. "You have a devious scheme in mind, Eudora. I can all but taste it."

"We shall see. It's true that I am of a mind to stir the pot, but it is far too soon for explanations. What is your opinion of the young gentleman, Jane? And pray, don't be missish."

He never noticed me, she thought immediately. *He looked right past me, as if I were of no consequence whatever.* That rankled more than she was willing to admit, even to Eudora. "His skin is very dark," she said slowly. "I would guess he has spent the past few years under a hot sun. He is used to being active. A small room, like this one, makes him feel trapped."

"Precisely. Go on, my dear."

She closed her eyes, recapturing him in her mind. "He was angry with you, of course, but even angrier with himself for letting it show. He put me in mind of an actor badly miscast in a role but determined to play it out."

"My impression exactly," Eudora said with approval. "He is a Fallon to the core, knows it, and cannot brook the idea."

"Do you mean licentious and corrupt, like his father?"

"No, indeed. But that incredible energy and impatience must be directed somewhere. His predecessor wore himself into the grave with gaming and whoring, and this one may well follow suit. But I suspect otherwise. It is my guess that he is resolved to become as virtuous as they were monstrous. A pity, that."

"However so? You would have him follow in their footsteps only to provide a new round of Fallon scandals for you to write about?"

"No, no, my dear." Eudora toyed with the fringe on her lap robe. "But nothing is more repellent than an aspiring saint who takes himself too seriously. A man requires a liberal seasoning of flaws, else he is like to grow critical and self-righteous. Besides, pattern cards make demmed poor company."

Jane laughed. "Not everyone maintains your exceptionally low standards, Eudora. If the marquess is bent on sanctity, I expect nothing will stand between him and canonization."

"He will not easily be deflected, that is certain."

Jane regarded her with foreboding. Eudora had got that febrile look in her eyes, the one that signaled trouble ahead. "I believe," she said carefully, "that his lordship is best left to make his way however he wishes. Will you consider removing the Fallons from your book?"

"Not at present. Should I yield to one such demand, I must, in all fairness, do the same for others who approach me with a similar request. Very soon, my dear, I'd be left with no book at all."

And a good thing, too, Jane thought. The history would be of interest, and perhaps of genuine importance, a century from now. But *Scandalbroth*? She couldn't fathom why Eudora had chosen to put the book in print. The notorious Lady Swann was already known to everyone of importance, and she cared nothing for public acclaim.

Nor, as she had told Fallon, was money a factor. She had more than she could spend if she lived another six-and-eighty years. Routinely she sent hefty donations to a score of charitable enterprises, and the enormous bequests in her will would endow more than one orphanage.

She had a good heart, Eudora, although she feigned otherwise. Jane had learned of her considerable generosity quite by accident and knew better than to speak of it. But why would a woman who helped so many people have set herself to injure so many others with her book?

Eudora had lusty appetites, a razor-edged tongue, and a shameless fondness for gossip, but an otherwise sterling character. Nobody is perfect, Jane reflected with a gulp. How well she knew!

She glanced up at Eudora, who seemed lost in her own thoughts—or, more likely, in some deplorable plot relating to the Marquess of Fallon. She often boasted that in all her years, after marrying and burying a half-dozen husbands, she had never met the man who could best her. Jane rather thought she'd not given up looking for one, if only for the excitement of vying with a will and intelligence that equalled hers.

Of course, since that was Jane's own secret longing, she was probably reading too much into Eudora's intentions.

"I mean to toy a bit with the toplofty Marquess of Fallon," Eudora announced into the silence.

Oh dear.

"It will do him good," she continued reflectively. "And since the book is all but completed, I am in need of diversion. Unfortunately, he is too much the fool to let me seduce him, although one night in my bed would be the making of the man."

Jane chuckled under her breath. In early days she had assumed that Eudora was jesting about her lovers, until the night she cracked her door open and watched an eager-looking gentleman about fifty years of age creep down the passageway to Eudora's bedchamber. Later a maidservant explained that the gentlemen were compelled to sneak in and out of the house to spare Felicia's delicate sensibilities. The ancient, loyal companion would pack up and leave if she knew of such goings-on right under her virginal nose.

"But I need to think on this scheme awhile longer." Eudora leaned forward in her chair to pat Jane's arm. "It may well be my greatest triumph, if I can put all the ducks in order. By Twelfth Night, Fallon will be dancing to my tune. See if he isn't!"

"Eudora, sometimes you positively terrify me." Jane stood, bent over to kiss a papery cheek, and went back to her desk. "Whatever you are up to, please don't tell me about it."

"Of course I will not," Eudora assured her. "That would spoil all the fun."

Chapter 2

Her arms overflowing with parcels, Jane smiled gratefully at the young man who hurried ahead of her to open
the shop door. Sweeping his hat from his head, he gave
her an exaggerated bow that set her to laughing as she
stepped into the bright cold afternoon.

All London brimmed with Christmas spirit, although it
was only the middle of December. Clerks had chatted
jovially as they tied string around her packages, fellow
shoppers asked her opinion of a length of ribbon or a
child's toy, and passers-by nodded greetings as they
dodged one another on the crowded pavement.

Jane caught the eye of a hackney driver, who pulled to
the curb where she stood, and was delighted when a
tradesman stopped to open the carriage door and let
down the steps. Such attention and kindness, she thought
as the cab rumbled slowly along the crowded street. This
must be everyone's favorite time of the year.

The closed compartment soon grew redolent with a
heady mixture of spicy fragrances. She'd bought packets
of ginger, cinnamon, nutmeg, cloves, raisins, and candied fruits, along with a book of receipts that she was
eager to try. Cook surely would not object, so long as she
used the kitchen only at odd hours of the day. She meant
to have a go at a Christmas pudding, Portugal cakes, and
gingerbread men.

A year ago the holidays had passed with scarcely a
ripple. Eudora, peevish because most of her acquaintances were gone to their country estates, had thrown

herself into dictating the first portion of *Scandalbroth*. They had even worked on Christmas Day.

But this time, Jane had promised herself, all would be different. She meant to decorate the house with holly and evergreen boughs, set a crèche on the mantelpiece, and choose special presents for everyone in the household.

Some might think a quiet holiday with only two elderly ladies and a few servants for company rather tedious, but this would be quite the best Christmas she'd ever had. She couldn't remember a time she had so looked forward to anything. At night she lay in bed selecting the gifts she would buy—a soft warm shawl for Felicia, she had decided, and perhaps a pair of fur-lined slippers for the cold evenings.

Eudora's present would be more difficult. What could she find that Lady Swann didn't already have? All the same she enjoyed roaming through the shops, hoping that something would catch her eye. She'd never before had enough money to indulge her secret passion for shopping, which had burst forth with a vengeance this very afternoon. She could scarcely wait for tomorrow's expedition.

Eudora was sitting by the fire when Jane burst into the parlor, two or three small parcels tumbling from her arms onto the carpet. She dropped the others on a side table and went back to retrieve the strays.

"About time!" Eudora snapped. "I've been waiting for you."

Jane glanced over her shoulder, relieved to see a smile on Eudora's face. A rather devious smile, she thought after a closer look. "Is it so very late? I lost track of time."

"Past three o'clock, you wretched child. And you know how impatient I become when I've news to share."

"Have you?" Jane threw herself on a chair and propped her aching feet on a leather ottoman. "Tell me all."

"Had a good time today, did you?" Eudora peered intently through her lorgnette. "I've never before seen your cheeks this flushed or your eyes so bright. You are remarkably pretty, Jane, when you are in high spirits."

Pretty? Astonished, Jane untied the ribbons of her bonnet. No one had ever used "pretty" and "Jane" in the same sentence, unless there was a "not" attached.

"It's true, you know. When you came to me, no meat on your bones, hair limp as a wet mop, I failed to recognize your potential. Oh, make no mistake, you'll never be an Incomparable. But you have a fine, shapely body and a vivacious, endearing nature. Yours is the sort of beauty a man rarely notices until compelled to take a good long look. From that time, he finds himself unable to look away."

And what brought *this* on? Jane wondered, beginning to unbutton her pelisse. "The only time I encounter men is when they come here to call on you, and nary a one has ever paid me the slightest attention. How could they, with you in the room?"

"True," Eudora said with a laugh. "I am formidable competition. You will be relieved to hear that I am about to take myself off for several weeks."

"But you *can't!*" Jane's hand clenched on a button, nearly ripping it loose. "I mean, where are you going?"

Eudora lifted a sheet of paper from her lap and waved it in the air. "The Duchess of York has invited me to spend Christmas at Oatlands Park! All the best people will be there—Alvanley, Monk Lewis, Brummell—and I suspect they mean to quiz me about *Scandalbroth*. Felicia will accompany me, but I'm afraid I cannot take you along this time."

"Of course not," Jane replied automatically, visions of her wonderful Christmas slipping away. "Ought you to travel so far, though? The roads will be terrible."

"Pah. I positively require a holiday from this house, however difficult the journey. Indeed, I don't believe I've left Upper Brook Street these last three years. Past time, wouldn't you say?"

"Certainly." Jane shaped her trembling lips into a smile.

"The adventure will do wonders for your spirits. I expect you will be the sensation of Her Grace's house party."

"There can be no doubt. What's more, the duchess is dispatching her own carriage to take me there. It must be a decade since I rode out in style, with liveried footmen and crests on the doors. Do you know, Jane, I feel like a mere girl of sixty again."

Although her heart was sinking, Jane couldn't help but share Eudora's excitement. And what was one more lonely Christmas, after all? She would bake gingerbread men and eat every last one of them herself.

"We leave tomorrow morning," Eudora said. "Felicia is packing my things, although later you might offer to help. She moves as if the air were made of molasses. No, no, don't get up now. We still have much to discuss."

Jane sank back on the chair and applied herself again to the buttons. Did Eudora mean to close down the house while she was away? Oh, dear Lord.

"I have told the servants to arrange a suitable schedule to visit their families and friends," Eudora said, "but one or two will always be in residence with you."

Jane nodded, relief flooding through her. At least she would have a place to stay. "I can do without servants, you know. Perhaps they should all take an extended holiday."

"Most have nowhere to go, my dear. Not for weeks at a stretch, in any case, and Cook may never leave the house at all. As for you, it's possible you may be kept so busy that you'll not miss me in the slightest."

"I can finish editing the book, of course. When you return, it will be all but ready for the publisher."

"Oh, never mind that!" Eudora waved a hand impatiently. "I've a new task for you, although it may come to nothing. And if that is the case, you must relax and forget *Scandalbroth* until my return."

Jane shrugged out of her pelisse, regarding Eudora suspiciously. She'd got that feverish look in her eyes again. "What do you wish me to do for you?" she inquired without enthusiasm.

"Ah, well, I imagine you will not leap at my proposal. But I do expect you to obey me. This has to do with the Marquess of Fallon."

"In wh-what way, ma'am?"

"*Ma'am?* Tsk tsk. You are in the boughs before I've even begun to explain." Eudora chuckled. "It has been a long time indeed since a man surprised me, but Fallon has done so. I assumed he would come back again to plead his case, but apparently he is even more stubborn than I imagined. Now it seems I must go to him. Or rather, *you* must do so in my stead, as I shall not be here to handle the business myself."

Why, Jane thought, the crafty old woman had *arranged* that invitation to Oatlands. Who but Eudora Swann could persuade a duchess to cooperate in such a manner! This had to be part and parcel of the scheme she mentioned the day Lord Fallon paid his call, but as she had said not another word on the subject in the two weeks since, Jane had reckoned she'd forgot all about it.

"You are thinking wicked thoughts, gel." Eudora tapped her fan on the arm of her chair. "All the same, you will hear me out. I shall dictate a letter explaining my proposal, and you may carry it to Fallon on the morrow. Despite your scowl, missie, you may find yourself pleased with what I mean to suggest."

"You will not publish *Scandalbroth*?"

"Let us say that I am reconsidering. Largely because you disapprove of the book, I must add."

"I have tried not to say so," Jane protested.

"Tried, yes. But in unguarded moments, what you are thinking is writ across your face, and I have seen your knuckles whiten as you pen my most salacious anecdotes. Your opinions are of considerable interest, even of value, but they cannot dissuade me. I refuse to be forgot, my dear. And as I've borne no children, a book must be my legacy."

"I do understand," Jane said earnestly. She had no children, either, nor any book to write. There would be for her no great passion, nor an abiding love. She often thought that Jane Ryder would pass through this world without leaving a single mark on it.

"Do attend me a few moments longer," Eudora scolded. "The letter will go into greater detail, but here in a nutshell is my proposal. While I require a book to put the seal on my reputation, it need not be *Scandalbroth*. The history will do well enough, and when 'tis opened—just imagine, in nineteen hundred and eleven!—I shall come to life again."

"I believe you are making a wise choice, Eudora."

"Ain't made it yet, missie. The history must be complete, accurate, and engrossing, but so far it's nothing of the sort. The Fallons will liven it up, I expect, if there is more to their tale than the shopworn escapades of the feckless marquesses. I wish to learn of their wives, and what became of the daughters, for there must have been one or two girl children in all those years." She tilted her head. "Unless I am much mistaken, this new lordling's story is the most fascinating of them all."

Jane recalled the hot-eyed, impatient man who had stalked the perimeters of this room, slapping his gloves against his thigh, now and again remembering his manners only to forget them again within seconds. Yes, he was indeed fascinating, but hardly a man to reveal his secrets even to Eudora, who could pry secrets from a rock. "I'd wager he will tell you nothing," she said.

"Not immediately," Eudora conceded. "All the same, he is a dealmaker, that one. I recognize his sort. He will trade information, you may be sure, on my promise to conceal it for a century. The alternative—Fallon scandals up for sale in the bookshops—he will find insupportable. 'Tis a fair bargain, Jane."

"Actually, I think he'd find it a far sight easier to simply murder you. And steal the only copy of *Scandalbroth* while he was about it."

"Ah, but he would have to murder you, too," Eudora pointed out. "Don't think I have failed to notice that you remember everything you read or hear. Let us see how he responds to my proposal, shall we?"

"Very well. But why must I deliver the letter personally? Can we not send it by post?"

"Oh, indeed no. I expect him to grant you access to the family papers and to dictate his own story to you. That means, of course, that he must take your measure, which will be a simpler matter if you are standing directly in front of him. And if he approves, you will have the next several weeks to begin compiling the Fallon history." Her eyes narrowed. "I am relying on you, Jane, to see this project through."

"And if he refuses?"

"Then you must change his mind. Let me give you a piece of advice, young woman. When dealing with Fallon, do not behave for a single moment in the manner of a secretary or a servant. You stand in my place, and you well know that I am not to be denied."

"No one on the planet can stand in your place, Eudora. And the fact is, I *am* a secretary and a servant."

She waved a hand. "Let us not refine too much on that, missie. I expect you to bring him around, whatever it requires you to do."

"Eudora," Jane said between clenched teeth, "you are incorrigible. Should his lordship set out to murder you, I rather think I shall offer to help him."

"That's my girl! Now go to your desk so that I may dictate the letter. Fallon has moved to a house in Berkeley Square, I understand. Tomorrow, when I am gone, you may call on him there."

Jane would as soon skip tomorrow, bypass Christmas, and slide directly into January. On leaden feet she made her way to the desk.

"Ah, wait!" Eudora cried. "I almost forgot. As I won't be here on Christmas morn, you shall have your presents this very moment. They are in the drawer beneath the window seat."

Jane whirled around. "You bought presents for *me*? Oh heavens, Eudora, I've scarcely begun my own shopping. I have nothing for you as yet."

"Just as well. You will find a new reticule among your gifts, and I have put into it enough money to purchase me a gewgaw. The rest will cover any extraordinary expenses you may encounter in my absence." Eudora wheeled closer to the window, her eyes alight with pleasure as Jane lifted a stack of boxes from the drawer.

She had never received a gift specially chosen for her. Sometimes her employers had provided an orange, sweetmeats, and handkerchiefs or gloves, but the other servants received exactly the same. She felt like an eager child as she reached first for the smallest box. It contained an exquisite watch, which would fit neatly into her pocket.

"Oh my," she whispered, eyes burning. "It's beautiful, Eudora."

"A trifle! Mere silver plate. Now you'll have no excuse to be late. Go on. Open them all."

The next box held gold earbobs in the shape of stars. There was a fur muff and buttery-soft kidskin gloves and warm woolen stockings. She exclaimed over each present, fighting back her tears as Eudora impatiently urged her to be quicker about the business. Before she came to the last box, she was surrounded by delicate handkerchiefs, silk stockings, two lacy night rails, and a tempting assortment of books to read.

Head spinning with joy, she tore into the largest of the boxes and lifted tissue paper from a carefully folded mound of bright crimson wool.

"It's a cloak," Eudora said. "Try it on."

Jane stood and swung the cape around her shoulders. It was exactly the right length, soft and full and deliciously warm, the lapels and hood lined with ermine.

"Oh, my word," she murmured, unable to hold back

27

her tears a moment longer. She flung herself at Eudora and embraced the old woman, sobbing uncontrollably.

"There, there, missie," Eudora murmured, stroking her head. "You've had few enough presents in your time, I warrant, but that's no reason to turn into a watering pot. I feel badly enough, leaving you alone at Christmas and sending you on an errand you would as soon forgo."

Jane lifted her head. "I don't mind. Truly."

"Yes, you do. But it's all for the best, if my instincts are still in working order, and they ain't failed me yet. Go to your desk now, m'dear, and sharpen your pen. We've a letter to write."

Chapter 3

Fallon crushed the sheet of paper in his hand and lobbed it into the trash basket. Some days he couldn't remember his own name.

He had inadvertently signed the letter "Rowan," the courtesy title by which he'd been known for nearly all his four-and-thirty years. As for Charles Everett Lawson Phillip Padgett, those were merely words on a parish registry in Essex. Not even his mother had ever called him Charles. From here on out, of course, he would bear the vile Fallon name and, most probably, a good part of the vile Fallon reputation.

Larch appeared in the doorway. "Luncheon is served, m'lord."

Fallon set his pen in the holder, stoppered the ink bottle, and followed his extremely proper butler to the dining room.

Like all the other rooms in his newly purchased town house, it was decorated with elegant furniture chosen by a hired expert in such matters. A polished mahogany table stretched out before him, long enough to seat thirty guests. At the very end, one place setting awaited his presence.

Two footmen and a maid were lined up by the sideboard, ready to take hot platters from the dumbwaiter and offer him more food than any ten men could possibly eat. A footman hurried to pour wine in the first of several glasses arrayed on the table.

A luncheon fit for a marquess awaited him. An expensive

French chef had prepared it. The agency that supplied his staff had also provided a wine steward to stock his cellar. All was exactly as it should be.

He found himself wanting to be seated cross-legged before a campfire, a crispy jungle fowl roasting on the spit, exchanging bad jokes and old stories with his friends.

In London he had no friends, no one to invite to his new house and his new table.

But things were about to change, he reminded himself while a servant pulled out his chair and opened his napkin, as if a marquess were incapable of doing so unassisted. Now he had a house in Berkeley Square, a fashionable wardrobe, and the most arrogant valet who ever ironed a neckcloth. He had bought the finest of everything, from horses to servants. He was ready to begin his new life.

Lobster bisque was dished into a shallow, gold-edged bowl, and the servants visibly relaxed when he tasted it and nodded approval. *They fear me,* he thought, amused. On the whole, he found the lot of them devilishly intimidating, especially Larch.

He felt like a great looby, putting away his soup with four pairs of eyes fixed on him. Well, not precisely fixed, for the servants were too well trained to stare. But they remained on full alert, in the event he looked as if he might want something. He'd have preferred a tray in his room, but knew he must keep up the standards expected of the new Marquess of Fallon. His predecessors had kept to standards that would shame a pigsty.

As the soup dish was removed and the next course set before him, he mentally rehearsed his plans for the day. Cards had been dispatched to anyone he could remember meeting whilst in India, and most had replied cordially. Now, armed with a list of people to call on, he meant to start with the ones who could do him the most good.

First up was Richard Wellesley, who had been governor-general of Bengal when they met some years ago. Now he served as foreign secretary under Perceval, and was doubtless kept busy indeed. But he'd expressed interest in seeing his old friend again, probably hoping Fallon would ally himself with Tory factions in the Lords. Wellesley rarely gave without expecting to receive. Nor, for that matter, did he.

They both knew how the game was played and would get on splendidly together.

Fallon speared a chunk of turbot and forked it into his mouth. With any luck Wellesley would propose him for membership in one or more of the clubs. That was his next goal, and his timing was all but perfect. In December, with nearly everyone of importance gone to the country, even the Fallon heir might survive the voting without a blackball.

He had resolved to sneak his way into Society, certain the direct approach, which better suited his nature, was doomed to failure. When he had set himself up as the model aristocrat, gained admission to the clubs, and hosted a series of impeccable parties at his impeccable town house, perhaps the beau monde would forget what they knew of his father.

But how could anyone forget, once that damned book hit the streets?

He put down his knife and fork with a clatter. No one could ruin an appetite like Lady Eudora Swann. His solicitor had confirmed the old crow's prediction that a lawsuit would generate a vast quantity of scandalous publicity and come to nothing in the end.

He still meant to find a way to stop publication, but two weeks of worrying at the problem had led him no closer to a solution. More than once he'd set out to confront her again but ended up turning back. What more was there to say, after all? And because Lady Swann was even more wealthy than she'd indicated, it was no good trying to throw money at her. Perhaps Wellesley, a master manipulator if ever there was one, could devise a practical scheme.

Fallon became aware the servants were regarding him apprehensively from the corners of their eyes, clearly wondering what had displeased him and what they ought to do about it.

Then all eyes swung to the door as a young footman stepped inside and bowed. Another footman, the one who had poured the wine, crossed the length of the room and accepted a whispered message. He came back and delivered the message in an undertone to the butler.

Devil it, somebody just tell me, Fallon thought as Larch took a step forward, a slight frown wrinkling his usually stiff face.

"A young woman asks to speak with you, my lord. She has come alone." That last word shivered with *meaning.* Larch drew himself even more erect. "Shall I send her away?"

"Well, that depends," Fallon replied, knowing he was supposed to have said yes. "Who is she?"

More murmuring between the footman and the butler. Larch shook his head as if he'd just learned that a rodent was waiting in the foyer. "She gave her name as Miss Ryder, my lord."

Fallon had never heard of Miss Ryder, but her timing was excellent. Now he had an excuse to leave this mausoleum of a dining room and a meal he no longer wanted.

"I'll see her," he said.

Jane stood alone in the enormous entrance hall where the footman had left her, gazing around curiously. She had never seen so much marble in all her life. The black-and-white checked floor, so highly polished she could see her reflection, felt cold through her leather half boots and woolen stockings. Marble statues, set in marble niches, lined the foyer. A sweeping marble staircase arced to a mezzanine overhead, where more marble statues were arrayed against the gold-leafed balustrade.

She tugged her brown woolen cloak around her, feeling as though she'd stumbled into an ice cave. What little color there was, from marquetry console tables and jade figurines, washed out against the dazzle of white stone. This was the sort of place where rich people were entombed, she thought. Nobody could actually *live* here.

At the last moment she had decided not to tell the footman she'd come on an errand for Eudora Swann. If Fallon refused to meet with the unknown Jane Ryder, she could then pass the letter to a servant and make her escape.

But this was not to be her lucky day. After several minutes, she heard the sound of boot heels striking marble. Lord Fallon appeared at the top of the staircase, pausing a moment to look down at her. Probably wondering who in blazes she was, Jane thought, remembering Eudora's instruction to hold her head high and meet the lofty Marquess of Fallon as an equal. Which was pure nonsense, of course.

She rather expected him to turn back and direct a servant to deal with that encroaching female, but he descended the stairs in full lord-of-the-manor fashion, an expression of aloof disinterest on his face.

He was as handsome as she remembered, but nothing else about him was the same. The tempestuous man who had stalked Eudora's parlor, afire with barely constrained energy, was gone. In his place stood a mannequin wearing a perfectly fitted blue tailcoat over pristine white linen. When he bowed, she belatedly remembered to bob a curtsy.

"Miss Ryder, I believe?" His voice was expressionless. "My apologies. You should not have been left to stand in the vestibule. Will you join me in the—" He glanced around as if uncertain where to go, a smile flickering across his lips. "I have only just moved into this house, and no one has thought to provide me with a map. Shall we explore the upper reaches in search of a parlor?"

Charm was the last thing she had expected from Lord Fallon. But it dissipated immediately when a skull-faced butler appeared, sniffing audibly at her plain brown cloak and wilted bonnet as he led them up the stairs.

"Would you care for refreshments?" Fallon inquired politely.

She speedily declined. "Thank you, my lord, but I shall require only a few moments of your time."

"As you wish." He dismissed the butler and gestured her to a chair near the fireplace. "How may I serve you, Miss Ryder?"

Jane perched on the edge of the chair, wishing he would sit down, too. But he stood near the mantelpiece, hands clasped behind his back, so perfectly poised and self-contained that he might as well have been one of the statues in his entrance hall. Why had he agreed to see her? There was no sign of recognition on his face, nor any hint of curiosity in his eyes.

With fingers that insisted on trembling, she opened her reticule. "I have a letter for you, Lord Fallon. From Lady Swann."

If she expected him to be surprised, she was disappointed. He only nodded, stepping forward to take the folded sheet of paper and moving back again to the fireplace where the light was better.

After recording Eudora's dictation in shorthand and neatly reinscribing the text on the paper he was reading, Jane knew every word of the letter by heart.

Lord Fallon,

As it is the season of kindness and generosity, I have given thought to your request that I exclude your family from my book. Would that it were easy to grant such a boon.

Alas, it is not within my power. My associate, Miss Ryder, will explain the reasons, although I am certain you understand them clearly enough. *Scandalbroth* must be published whole or not at all, and the thought of departing this world without bestowing upon it a legacy of my own is insupportable.

However, I have also assembled another book, something of a history of the aristocracy for the past seventy years, which will be filed away and released a century from now. Because this volume is not focused on scandalous doings, the Fallons scarcely appear at all.

Should you agree to release for Miss Ryder's inspection all information and documents relating to your family, and if she can thereby compile a history to my satisfaction, there is a possibility I shall consider foregoing *Scandalbroth* altogether.

While I am away, Miss Ryder will be free to examine your records. And on my return, in light of what you have provided her, I shall make my final decision.

Happy Holidays, Lord Fallon.

Yrs, etc.,

Lady E. Swann

For the briefest moment, flames seemed to leap from Fallon's eyes. But she must have imagined it, because within seconds he was perfectly composed again. Only the slightest lift of his aristocratic eyebrow, a gesture more telling than he probably knew, betrayed any emotion whatever.

"Rubbish," he said in a level voice. "*A possibility* that she will *consider*? Does she expect me to take seriously this alleged offer of a compromise?"

Jane thought it a rhetorical question, but his steady gaze remained focused on her, and the eyebrow was still arched. Good Lord, who was *she* to speak for Eudora Swann, never mind that Eudora had sent her here to do precisely that.

Jane gave him a noncommittal smile. "Lady Swann says little she does not mean, my lord. The offer is as genuine as the escape routes she has provided for herself, should she decide the Fallon history to be of insufficient interest."

"On the contrary. This is an underhanded ploy to wring

access to information she cannot acquire by legitimate means, which she will proceed to use without the smallest concern for anyone but herself."

"Unfair! You leap to judgment, sir. You do not know her."

"I recognize her kind," he said derisively. "I've dealt with any number of them over the years. At times I have used similar tactics myself . . . but only when dealing with fools. Does Lady Swann think me a fool, Miss Ryder?"

"She has not said so, Lord Fallon. Has she reason to believe it?"

His lips twitched but quickly hardened again. "I suspect she has long since decided that all men are fools. And like everyone else, she expects me to follow in the inglorious footsteps of my ancestors."

"People will judge you for what you are," she said, thinking how inane that sounded even as the words came from her mouth. With a tiny sigh, she tried again. "I am familiar with every scandalous tale in the book, and you are nothing like any of the Fallon marquesses described there."

"Am I not?" His eyebrow arched once more. "You are guessing, Miss Ryder, and that is not a wise thing to do. Anyone who ever trusted a Fallon has paid for it. For all you know, I mean to present a false image of myself to lure ingenuous pigeons into my trap."

"Which is precisely what you accuse Lady Swann of doing with this letter. Perhaps the two of you are well matched." She stood, straightening her skirts. "I'd as soon not be caught in the middle, my lord. If you do not intend to comply with her proposal, I must be on my way."

"I do not." He lifted a hand. "But tell me, please, how it is you have associated yourself with a filthy-minded old woman and her revolting book. You do not seem the type."

She couldn't help but grin. "Perhaps I, too, am presenting a false image. To be perfectly honest, my lord, I greatly enjoyed every story she told me about your family. Most were rather pedestrian—the usual drinking, gaming, and wenching—but now and again, your ancestors were amazingly inventive."

"That's quite enough! You would do well to seek better employment, young woman."

"And you would be astonished, sir, to learn how few choices females have when seeking employment. I much prefer taking dictation about vice than being compelled to experience it for myself."

He flushed hotly. "Forgive me. I didn't mean to read you a lecture. Well, obviously I did mean to, but I had no right. Certainly you need not be caught up in my quarrel with Lady Swann. Where can she be found?"

"She did not give me leave to reveal her direction, sir."

"Trust me, I can find out."

"No doubt. But you will only do yourself harm by going there. How will it look to the assembled company, and I assure you she is among excellent company indeed, if you swoop down upon an elderly lady in a wheeled chair and make a scene? It will be better if you accost her privately, on her return to London."

"And when will that be?"

"Not for several weeks, I believe. She expects me to research your family history in the meantime, but clearly you do not mean to cooperate. Good day, Lord Fallon."

Jane started for the door, head high, pleased to escape this unnerving man with her dignity intact. The rest of her had not fared so well. She felt uncommonly warm, and sharp little fingers seemed to be clawing at her from the inside out.

Before she was halfway across the parlor, he caught up and held out his arm. "I will show you to the door," he said.

What had been merely overheated and agitated became scorching and panicky. She stumbled on the smooth carpet and felt his muscles tighten as his arm supported her. He was kind enough to say nothing.

The silence lasted all the way down the marble stairs and into the entrance hall, where the formidable butler stood like an irate fence post.

Fallon drew her to a halt several feet away and leaned forward, speaking very softly at her ear. "Thank you for bringing the letter, Miss Ryder. If I offended you, be sure my temper was solely directed at your employer."

His hair brushed her cheek. She felt that light, intimate touch all the way to her toenails. And because it startled her, she withdrew her arm and quickly stepped away.

"I understand, sir." She curtsied. "And I wish you a very pleasant Christmas and a happy New Year."

Chapter 4

When Mr. Milhouse completed his report, his reedy voice faltering at the end, Fallon leaned forward in his chair and propped his elbows on the desk.

"Is there any *good* news?" he inquired mildly.

"I'm afraid not, my lord. You'll want to review the details in this file, of course, but I have given you a fairly accurate summation. Wolvercote is all to rack and ruin."

As he'd expected, Fallon thought, wondering why he had nonetheless cherished a futile hope that something of worth could be salvaged. But the estate was a shambles twenty years ago, when last he saw it, with only a few families still working the land to provide for themselves. His father had ignored their presence on the rare occasions he came up from London to sell off more of his heritage to pay his gaming debts. "What became of the tenant farmers?" he asked. "And the servants?"

"I have been unable to discover that, my lord. The house itself was abandoned not long after his lordship's demise, and we cannot determine when the last of the tenants fled. It must have been some years ago, given the condition of their cottages and the land, but no one remains to answer our many questions."

Fallon opened the file and scanned the first few pages of the investigators' report. "What of the woman mentioned here? Agathy Bligh. What has she to say?"

"Not a word, I'm afraid. Country folk are generally mistrustful of strangers, especially Londoners, and she has no legal right to be in the cottage where she is living now. I daresay she thought my clerks had come to evict her, because she would not let them through the door." Milhouse polished his spectacles with a handkerchief. "Do you wish me to see to it?"

"Certainly not. She is doing no harm." Fallon sifted through the thick sheaf of papers. "Is there a map somewhere in here? I require the precise location of every building on the estate, and what lies just beyond the boundaries in all directions."

"Forgive me, my lord. I should have thought of that." The solicitor mopped his damp brow. "I shall immediately dispatch surveyors and have a detailed map in your hands by Wednesday next."

"It can wait until the New Year, Milhouse. After all this time, another week's delay is of little consequence. But where did your people reside when they were inspecting Wolvercote? I had thought the house to be uninhabitable."

"So it is. Even the dower house, which was far better maintained, stands in need of considerable repair. By the way, someone has been staying there quite recently, although I surmise it was only a vagrant seeking temporary shelter. As for lodging, my employees made use of a small inn several miles from the estate. You'll find the name and direction in the files."

Fallon rose and swept the thick folder from the desk. "You have done well, Milhouse. I'll take this report to study and meet with you again after the first of the year."

When Fallon reached the outer office, a clerk stood waiting with his coat, hat, and gloves. And while he took a moment to put them on, the young man dashed ahead of him into the street, whistling for the carriage that waited around the corner.

These days, Fallon reflected moodily, people tripped over themselves to perform even the most unnecessary services. He was not at all sure he liked it. Hell, he'd made his fortune knowing where to go before others even guessed to go there and risked his life a hundred times to do what no one else dared to do.

Waiting around for servants grated on his nerves. He was used to being active, and this business of remaking himself into a man of leisure was proving to be damnably hard work. No doubt someone would even hold an umbrella over his head while he walked the few yards through the afternoon drizzle to the street.

Someone did. And tried to give him the umbrella, too, on the chance he might have need of it later.

Money changed everything, he reflected as his crested coach rumbled along the crowded street, and it would change him, too. But there was no point wondering if that was for good or ill. He had worked for two decades to arrive at this point and would be equally relentless until every last goal he'd set himself was achieved.

The carriage shuddered to a halt. "Cabbage wagon overturned directly ahead," the driver called. "We'll be stuck here fer a bit, m'lord."

Chuckling, Fallon leaned back against the plush leather squabs and crossed his ankles on the opposite bench. What use were a lofty title and a vast fortune, he thought, when a cabbage wagon stood in the way?

In any event, he'd nowhere important to go. Richard Wellesley had got him voted into White's, and another comrade from India days saw him admitted to Watier's, but there was little reason to hang about reading newspapers and sipping brandy when everyone of importance had left for the country. Until Parliament reconvened, London would be a social wasteland.

In his opinion Christmas was a dratted nuisance. He chafed to get on with the restoration of Wolvercote, but even the architects he planned to interview would not return to the city before Twelfth Night. What the devil was he going to do with himself for the next two weeks?

He could go to Wolvercote himself, he supposed, and have a look around. He'd meant to do that anyway, and this was as good a time as any. Even so, the prospect of setting foot in the house where he was born sent shivers

41

down his back. He'd loathed the place when he lived there and had no reason to love it now.

How had his mother felt, he wondered, when her new husband left her at the remote estate to give birth with only the servants in attendance? She had died shortly before his sixth birthday, and he had few memories of her. But even after he was sent away to school, he had nightmares in which she screamed his name. She had not been calling for him, he learned years later from a maidservant. Lady Fallon had been crying out from the pain of delivering two stillborn infants and miscarrying another.

Those events must have taken place years apart, but he recalled only one endless, desperate scream and wondered if it still echoed down the bleak passageways of Wolvercote. Hell confound it, he'd sooner face a charge of Maratha cavalry than walk alone into his own home.

Rarely introspective, he gave himself a mental kick on the backside. The past was exactly that—over and done with. Everything would be different when he brought his wife to the new Wolvercote.

For one thing, he would make certain to wed a female with a great many siblings. A woman born of a prolific mother was likely to produce children with relative ease, the same way mares of good stock could be relied on to deliver high-quality foals. And, too, she would have the best care money could provide. If necessary, he would employ a physician-in-residence and a swarm of nurse-maids to attend her every need.

Beyond that, he could not imagine. He knew only how to earn the funds to buy what he wanted. Once all was in place—house, wife, and children—where would *he* be? What would he do next?

More to the point, what should he do for the rest of the afternoon, if ever that blasted cabbage wagon was hauled out of his way?

Too bad Lady Swann, like everyone else, had run off to

celebrate Christmas away from London. He was in the mood to go another round with her about that pernicious book. She had all but tried to blackmail him, damn her eyes. And she bloody well knew that an upstart nobleman could not wrangle publicly with an eighty-six-year-old icon. But his pride would not admit the possibility of compromise, and he expected that the old bird would accept nothing short of total capitulation.

Only a saphead would have been taken in by her transparent plot, and she had mistaken her man if she thought him a fool. Not one shred, not one morsel of Fallon history would he hand into her keeping. His life in India was a closed book where she was concerned. And as for the future, Lady Swann would be unable to snoop out a wisp of scandal attached to him, for the simple reason that there would be none. He had resolved to become the perfect aristocrat if it killed him.

It occurred to him that he had been permitting Lady Swann to call the tune. She already knew a great deal about the Fallons and had only to interrogate people he'd known in India to gather information about him. If they were to do battle, which seemed inevitable, he ought to adopt a few of her tactics. Know his enemy, for example, and carry the attack into her camp. Best of all, she had inadvertently given him both the opportunity and the weapon, in the person of Miss Jane Ryder.

The more he thought about it, the more he liked his idea. If he took her to Wolvercote, pretending to offer access to family records, he wouldn't have to go there alone. Not that he required company to inspect an empty old house, of course. No, Miss Ryder's companionship was quite unnecessary, and she would probably prove a terrible nuisance.

But he could put up with her for a few days, if only to uncover information about Lady Swann and determine how best to exploit her weaknesses. She would find nothing of use at Wolvercote, that was certain. Records and family letters would long since have been devoured by mice or used to kindle fires.

Yes, it was a foolproof plan . . . so long as Miss Ryder agreed to come along. It would be best, he realized, to give her no time to think it over or apply to Lady Swann for further instructions. Instead, he would insist they travel right away—tomorrow at the latest—and compel her to decide immediately.

When the carriage began moving again, he directed the coachman to Upper Brook Street.

An ancient footman, in danger of toppling over when he bowed, looked surprised to see a caller on the door-stoop. "Lady Swann is not to home," he croaked.

"I am aware of that," Fallon said, moving past him into the vestibule. "It is Miss Ryder I wish to see."

"Well, sir, as to that, she is not receiving callers this afternoon. I expect she'll be available—"

"If she's here, she is available now. Where will I find her?"

A skinny finger pointed to a staircase at the end of the passageway. "She'll be in the kitchen, I expect."

Halfway down the stairs, Fallon smelled the distinct odor of something burning and followed threads of smoke to an open door. Beside a large butcher table, gazing down unhappily at something he could not see, stood Jane Ryder.

Strands of light brown hair had pulled loose from the knot at her nape to hang in limp strings over her flour-smudged cheeks. She brushed her hands against an apron three sizes too large for her slender body. "Poor fellows," she murmured. "I have incinerated the lot of you."

"Precisely who have you been tormenting this time, Miss Ryder?"

With a gasp, she looked up at him, then down at her filthy apron, and immediately began to brush at her hair with her fingertips.

The startled, feminine gesture made him almost sorry he had intruded, and also very glad of it. He moved closer and saw a number of blackened shapes on a baking sheet, smoke curling from their edges.

"They were supposed to be gingerbread men," she said with a rueful laugh. "That's my fourth batch. The other unfortunate creatures are equally charred, I fear, and the workings of this oven continue to elude me. Every adjustment I make to the fire only produces a greater catastrophe."

Fallon located one gingerbread man slightly less petrified than the others, broke off what was probably meant to be an arm, and popped it in his mouth. "Excellent flavor," he ruled. "The oven is clearly at fault for over-cooking them."

"And I am Marie Antoinette! Come, sir, why have you accosted me at my moment of baking despair? I clearly recall directing Mr. Mantooth to turn away all callers."

"Mr. Mantooth tried. But I wanted to speak with you today."

"Oh." She turned to the fire, and he had to strain to hear her voice. "I was just about to brew a pot of tea, Lord Fallon. If you will go upstairs to the parlor, I shall join you in a few minutes."

Despite the smoke and the acrid smell of burnt biscuits, he rather liked the warm homeyness of the kitchen. "Why don't we have tea here?" he suggested, stripping off his gloves and greatcoat.

"If you prefer. Do you mind if I clean up this mess before Cook sees it and rings a peal over my head?"

"Not in the least. Go about your business, Miss Ryder, while I explain why I have come." He was suddenly glad that her back remained turned as she measured tea leaves into a ceramic pot. At least he would not be lying to her face. "After some thought, and with little confidence in the results, I have decided to accept Lady Swann's offer. So, if you still wish to examine the family records, I shall provide access to whatever may remain at Wolvercote."

"I see." She poured steaming water from a kettle into

the teapot. "Wolvercote is the Fallon estate, as I recall. Will this access require me to go there personally?"

"Yes indeed. I've no intention of lifting a finger on Lady Swann's behalf. But I confess you'll not find this a pleasant outing, Miss Ryder. From the report of agents who have recently examined the property, it is in wretched condition. I have not yet seen it for myself."

"Truly?" She turned, regarding him curiously. "I'd have thought your home would be the first place you'd go."

"As it happens, I was saving it for last. But with London thin of company over Christmas, I've little else to do but inspect the ruins. If you are of a mind to sift through the rubble in search of Fallon history, I shall make what arrangements I can for your comfort. There is an inn, I understand, not far from the estate."

He watched her place cups, saucers, silverware, and napkins on a trestle table, nibbling all the while at her lower lip. What was she thinking, he wondered, when she frowned at a saucer of butter and set a crock of honey on the table with a decided clunk?

What was there to think about, after all? He had simply accepted the very offer she delivered to him a week ago—ah! *That* was it. By now Christmas was only three days away, and she likely had plans for the holiday.

With regret, he bid farewell to his scheme. He could scarcely pursue his own goals if it meant ruining her Christmas. "This can all wait until after the New Year, Miss Ryder."

"But you did not mean it to wait, I am convinced." She poured tea through a strainer into his cup. "There is no reason to postpone your trip on my account. Do you take milk? Pardon me. I do not and neglected to put it on to heat."

"Neither milk nor sugar, thank you."

Her smile lit up the kitchen. "As you see, I am as poor a hostess as I am a baker. Will you be seated, please? Cook made these scones for breakfast, and you cannot help but approve of them." She set a plate beside the teapot. "When would we depart, my lord? And how long would we be gone?"

She really meant to join him! Elated, he took a raisin-studded scone and broke it in half. "Would tomorrow be too soon? You can return the day after and be home in time for Christmas."

"Tomorrow will be fine." She sat across from him and filled her own teacup. "I am glad you changed your mind, sir. And Lady Swann will be pleased that I did not wholly waste my time while she was gone."

"Is she a difficult employer?"

She glanced at him in surprise. "If she were, I'd hardly say so. But in fact, she has been exceedingly kind. There is little I would not do for her in return."

Including this benighted journey to Wolvercote, he thought with a shot of guilt. While he respected her loyalty, it would better suit his purposes if she had an ax to grind. "I trust Lady Swann will appreciate your uncomfortable journey to an unpleasant destination on her behalf, especially if you return empty-handed." He slathered butter over a piece of scone. "The Fallons have been rather too preoccupied with their own vices to record them, or anything else, for posterity."

"She will recognize your willingness to cooperate, in any event. But that is unlikely to affect her decision about *Scandalbroth*."

"Is the manuscript here in the house?"

Her brows shot up in alarm. "I warn you, sir. You will get at anything belonging to Lady Swann only over my dead body."

"How ferocious of you." He couldn't help but laugh. "Do relax and enjoy your tea, Miss Ryder. I've come home to salvage what remains of the Fallon legacy and restore the family reputation, which pretty much rules out robbery and murder. Unfortunately. I'd certainly like to make off with every copy of that obscene book."

"Well, you cannot." She stirred honey into her tea. "And I won't tell you what's in it, either, so you needn't bother to ask. If I go with you to Wolvercote, it will be to acquire information, not to give it out."

He took another bite of scone, acknowledging silently that his Grand Plan was apparently doomed from the start. Jane Ryder had taken his measure, divined what he was up to, and put him on notice that it wouldn't work. She was gazing at him through lowered lashes as she sipped her tea, probably expecting him to call off the trip now.

Instinct told him that he was faced with a woman as strong-willed and intelligent as any man he had ever met. He'd felt a similar awareness of encountering someone beyond the ordinary a dozen years ago, when first introduced to Colonel Arthur Wellesley.

Prim Jane Ryder and the commander of the Peninsular Army! Fallon chuckled under his breath. But then, he'd few women among his acquaintance, and she could hardly be measured against one of his former mistresses. No, she was quite different from most females, conventional or otherwise. And for that reason, he determined to stay more than ever on his guard.

Despite his whirling thoughts, the companionable silence as they ate scones and drank tea was oddly pleasant. He found himself licking butter from his fingertips and wondered what Larch the butler would have thought. Guiltily he looked up at Jane Ryder. She was licking butter from her own fingers.

"I love sweets," she confessed with a grin. "These scones are wonderful, but you should taste Cook's blackberry pudding. It's fluffy as a cloud and positively melts in your mouth. She taught me how to make it, but I'm afraid my version was more suitable for paving roads. Nearly as bad as my gingerbread men, who were clearly destined to be roof shingles."

"In that case, we should take them with us. Wolvercote will require a new roof."

Her grin widened. "If it also requires new walls, I

could bake up a large batch of shortbread squares. The last time I did so, they had the consistency of bricks."

"If the results are so unsatisfactory, why the deuce do you keep trying to bake?"

"Oh, well, if failure could stop me, I'd never accomplish anything at all. You see, I perversely want to do precisely the things for which I have no talent whatever, like cooking and embroidery and learning other languages. Latin required five years, Greek seven, and I still don't trust my own translations."

He busied himself with a second scone to conceal his surprise. Why would a servant struggle to teach herself the classical tongues? Of what use were Latin and Greek to *any* female?

And how could she so easily make jokes about her gingerbread shingles and shortbread walls? He had no sense of humor whatever when he failed. To his mind, a man should successfully complete whatever he began. He supposed that applied to women, too, although women's work was mostly inconsequential. The world would go on perfectly well without embroidery, in his opinion.

"What are your real talents?" he heard himself ask.

"Oh, I've none that would interest you. They don't even interest me very much, however useful they may be on occasion. What comes easily offers no challenge, you see, and I am partial to challenges. Which is fortunate, because . . ."

As her voice faded, her wide hazel eyes lost some of their spark.

She had been about to reveal something of herself and swiftly thought better of it. With a sudden shot of awareness, he knew that if she ever fully trusted anyone, she would give over her heart and soul.

And soon regret it, he thought cynically. God protect her from him, and any man like him.

"Shall we settle the details of our trip?" he suggested in a level voice. "Can you be ready to depart tomorrow morning?"

"Certainly." Her tone was equally businesslike. "What time? And what shall I bring with me?"

Devil if he knew. When he decided to go somewhere, he up and went. "Wolvercote is about two hours from London, with good weather and decent roads, but we can count on neither at this time of year. What is more, I understand the last section of road will not accommodate my carriage. You may be forced to travel in a smaller vehicle."

"Fine with me," she said cheerfully. "We'll improvise. That's one of my talents, by the way. I'm good at improvisation."

"Well, so am I," he said, unaccountably pleased to find common ground with her. "Someone will collect you here at nine o'clock. I shall go on ahead, perhaps tonight, and secure rooms at the inn." Standing, he pulled on his greatcoat and picked up his gloves. "Are you likely to change your mind, Miss Ryder?"

"No, my lord. I am quite looking forward to having an adventure."

He snatched another scone from the platter on his way to the door. "Let us hope this proves to be nothing of the sort, young woman. I mean to have you home safe and sound before Christmas."

Chapter 5

The Black Dove had fallen on hard times.

A small, half-timbered building in the Tudor style, the inn had stood for centuries in this isolated place. But now, with Wolvercote abandoned, there were no servants and tenant farmers to while away an evening in the cozy taproom.

Since arriving that morning, Fallon had learned a good deal more about the inn's history and its current travails than he cared to know. Rollin Wilkens, the proprietor, rushed out to greet his guest as if the marquess had flown in on angel wings and introduced the large clan of Wilkenses one by one, assuring his lordship they would be at his service day and night.

Clinging like burrs, more like. Hoping for privacy, Fallon chose to take luncheon in his bedchamber, but one or another Wilkens kept finding an excuse to stop in. The youngest daughter, a flirtatious minx of fourteen or so, had plumped his bed pillows and straightened the canopy drapes half a dozen times.

The price of tonight's lodging, it appeared, was accepting responsibility for a score of good-natured Wilkenses. He could not help but appreciate their strategy. This was a desperate family grasping at a lifeline, and he was it.

" 'Twill need a heap of work," Rollin Wilkens was saying about Wolvercote as he cleared dishes from his lordship's meal. "The gentlemen what stayed here while they was examinin' the remains, so to speak, thought it likely oughter to be rebuilt from the ground up."

After a sleepless night going over the report, Fallon already knew to expect the worst. "What is the condition of the road?"

"Oh, no road from here." Wilkens brushed crumbs from the small table. "Not even a track can be seen, what with the snow. You'll have to go by horse through the forest and the fields. If you want, I'll sketch a map."

"Do. It may prove useful at some point. But Miss Ryder is traveling in my curricle, so we shall be forced to go in by the main road. Is it a great distance from here?"

"Well, let me see. Two miles from here to the post road, and five more to where you'd turn onter the estate road. But I much doubt that's fit for travel, except by horse. Nobody's used it since yer father died, and not many before then. Better to go from here, I 'spect. 'Tis only three miles, even with all the meandering." Wilkens grinned over yellow, broken teeth. "You chose the right place to stay, milord. Now, what else can I bring you? Wine? Good country ale?"

"Nothing more, except the map. Have you a horse and sidesaddle for hire?"

Wilkens guffawed. "Not likely, m'lord. We've a mule what pulls our cart, when he's of a mind to. If we gots to go somewheres, we mostly walks."

"I see." Fallon had a mental vision of himself twenty years ago, hitching rides on dung wagons and tramping for miles in his worn boots, on blistered feet. He knew very well how it was to be poor, far better than he knew how to be rich. "Thank you, Wilkens. I may snatch a nap until the others arrive, so—"

"We won't be botherin' you," Wilkens assured him, carrying an armload of dishes to the door. "You call down the stairs if you be needin' somethin' more."

Blessedly alone, Fallon crossed to the window and leaned his shoulder against the casement. His room overlooked the front of the inn, and he could see the tracks of his horse on the narrow, winding path that led to the courtyard.

Otherwise the landscape beyond the low stone wall lay pristine as a virgin's night rail. The pale winter sun shone down from a clear sky, conjuring diamonds in the snowy fields. From the dark branches of trees, melting icicles hung like golden fingers in the reflected sunlight.

For a few moments he savored the quiet beauty of an English country winter. It reached to places inside himself he had long since forgot in the stifling heat and crowded streets of Calcutta. He tried to relax, empty his mind, and enjoy the peaceful solitude.

But he could never abide waiting. Before very long he was pacing the narrow borders of his room, pausing by the window each time he passed in hopes of seeing his curricle appear on the horizon.

At last he caught a glimpse of something in the far distance—something ominously red, like blood on the snow. It was moving, however slowly, and after a while he could discern a black smudge by its side.

Probably another of the Wilkens brood, he thought, watching the figure pause and shift the burden from one hand to the other. Soon the black smudge changed sides again, but this time, the figure raised an arm and removed something from its head. Light brown hair gleamed in the sunlight.

Fallon struck his forehead with the palm of his hand. Jane Ryder! Seconds later he was outside and running down the path. She had resumed her journey, but stopped again when she saw him pounding in her direction.

As he drew closer, he realized that she was wearing a scarlet cape and carrying a small portmanteau. The snow reached almost to the tops of her brown half boots. To his horror, she curtsied as he approached.

For some reason, that made him angry. "Why are you on foot?" he demanded. "Where the devil is the curricle? The driver? Where is my valet?"

She dropped the portmanteau and stretched her cramped

fingers. "Perhaps with the devil, sir, for I certainly wished them there more than once this morning. Well, not the curricle, which was an innocent bystander. It is currently mired in a snowbank, poor thing, with a broken something-or-t'other."

"I see," he said, not seeing at all. He was too astonished by this extraordinary female who seemed not the least bit put out by her ordeal. Her nose, cheeks, and lips glowed pink from the exertion of her walk, and her hazel eyes positively sparkled. She looked healthy and energetic, like a young doe romping in the snowfields without a care in the world. "You came to no harm in the accident, I apprehend."

"None whatever. Which is surprising because I landed directly atop Mr. Latmore, who is excessively bony. He maintains that I crushed the very life from his body." She laughed. "It must have been his ghost went on fretting after his demise."

In Fallon's own experience, Latmore never ceased complaining. "He is irritating, I agree, but a skilled valet nonetheless."

"So he informed me, although he omitted the 'irritating' part. That much I figured out for myself."

"Shall we continue on while you tell me what happened?" Fallon picked up the portmanteau she had been carrying, surprised at how heavy it was.

"Books," she explained when he looked a question at her. "I never go anywhere without something to read." She fell in step beside him, practically bouncing as she walked. "What a glorious day. The driver swears a storm is blowing in. He says that his knees tell him when the weather is about to change for the worse, but I cannot credit it. There isn't a cloud in the sky. And, too, he enjoys complaining nearly as much as Mr. Latmore. They engaged in a battle of personal woes the entire morning."

They would certainly have something to be woeful

about when next he saw them. "The accident?" he reminded her.

"Well, we had turned off the post road and gone perhaps a quarter mile when the right wheel suddenly broke away. Next I knew, Mr. Latmore and I were tumbled into a gully. When we'd scrambled back to the road, the pair of them began arguing what to do next. The driver wanted to unhitch the horses and lead them to a post house we had passed some miles back. Mr. Latmore insisted that your luggage could not be left without someone to guard it."

"Do you mean that sapskull is now standing watch over my shirts and cravats?"

"Oh, hardly." She laughed. "You have forgot his poor, broken body, sir. Mr. Latmore proclaimed himself in dire need of a soft bed and a quick infusion of laudanum, which could only be had in a civilized place. Fortunately, he was strong enough to climb aboard one of the horses. I was instructed to wait with the curricle until they sent someone to retrieve your cases. But as you plainly see, I declined the honor."

"I should hope so. But *cases*? I told Latmore to pack only a few necessities."

"Your necessities occupy three cases, sir. The driver protested, but Mr. Latmore demanded they be strapped to the curricle. Naturally, the driver maintains that the excessive weight caused the accident, while Mr. Latmore attributes it to the cow-handed imbecile holding the reins. They were debating the subject when last I saw them."

Fallon, furious at the treatment accorded this slip of a girl, resolved to discharge the men without a reference. "They should have taken you with them to the post house."

"I'd not have gone, sir. Indeed, I was supremely glad to be rid of them both. The driver will see your curricle repaired, but we cannot expect it to arrive today. Meantime, I took the liberty of opening your cases and have

55

brought along a few items you may need. Actually, I started out carrying two cases, but was forced to abandon one along the way. A year in London with so little exercise has turned me up soft."

Hardly that, he thought, more than a little impressed with this unusual female. He'd never met anyone like her. And he was not at all sure how to deal with her, which made him excessively uncomfortable. In her company, words seemed to stick in his throat. "I am used to traveling light," he said to no purpose whatever. "You needn't be concerned on my account."

"Oh, I'm not," she said immediately. "You aren't paying me to take care of you, after all. But it was no trouble to add your shaving kit, shirts, and a dressing gown to my own case. I was unable to find a nightshirt."

Because he always slept in the altogether, a fact he wasn't about to confide. "Thank you," he said, relieved to see the inn directly ahead. "You must be tired and hungry. I shall have a meal and a hot bath sent to your bedchamber. It is rather small, I fear, and somewhat primitive."

She stepped into the paneled vestibule and gazed around with obvious pleasure. "How very lovely. This building must be hundreds of years old."

Rollin Wilkens darted from the taproom. "Foundation was laid in 1570," he announced proudly. "Mrs. Wilkens has just prepared a venison stew, milady. We'll take good care of you."

Fallon handed him the portmanteau and watched Miss Ryder follow Wilkens up the stairs. Then he wandered into the taproom, where a mug of ale was quickly put in his hand.

All his plans had unraveled, except that Jane Ryder had managed to arrive intact. But she would require the afternoon and evening to recover, which made their trip to Wolvercote out of the question. He could, of course, go there on his own. That was certainly the most practical thing to do. But he accepted a refill of ale and remained on the bar stool, the muscles in his body taut as bowstrings.

Wolvercote. *Alone.*

He could not make himself stand up and go.

Jane declined Mr. Wilkens's offer of a hot bath, as she'd had one before daybreak that very morning. A pitcher of water, basin, and sponge did well enough, and she was soon working her way through a large bowl of venison stew and chunks of toasted bread-and-cheese.

Less than half an hour after entering the small bed-chamber, she wrenched her hair into a tight knot and snatched a final look in the small mirror on her dressing table. Neat and respectable, just as she ought to be. But her plain, long-sleeved dress of hunter green kerseymere was new, and she'd had few enough new dresses in her lifetime to relish the pleasure of wearing one.

She felt exhilarated from her walk that morning, nearly as charged with energy as Fallon always seemed to be. A year spent mostly in Eudora's overheated house had been rather stifling, although she was certainly grateful for a safe roof over her head, regular meals, and congenial company. If she caught herself wishing for more, a mental kick sent the intrusive thoughts skittering away.

And now for Lord Fallon, whose arrangements for this journey had gone badly awry. He was displeased, she knew, and impatient to get on about his business. She checked her new watch, which showed a little past one o'clock, and decided they had almost three hours before sunset. That should be enough time for a preliminary look-in at Wolvercote.

She had not reckoned on the complications.

"One h-horse?"

"I'm afraid so. Forgive my abominable planning, Miss Ryder. I have wasted your time and spoiled your Christmas holiday. When the driver returns with the curricle, I shall instruct him to carry you back to London with all due speed."

"I don't mind walking to Wolvercote, you know." She glanced at the crude pencil-drawn map spread before him on the bar. "Is it a terribly long way?"

"Three miles, I believe, but you cannot be permitted to walk such a distance." He regarded her speculatively. "Could you remain aboard my horse without a sidesaddle while I walk ahead, holding the reins?" He brushed a drop of ale from the map. "Unless you'd be willing to ride double, but I suppose—"

"Then it's settled!" she interrupted before he could talk himself out of the obvious solution. "We should leave immediately, sir, if you wish to accomplish anything this afternoon. I'll retrieve my cloak and meet you at the stable."

Chapter 6

Fallon guided Scorpio through a copse of oak and up a steep rise, only to see yet another bare snowy hill on the other side. According to Rollin Wilkens's map, they should long since have arrived at Wolvercote.

A sudden rush of cold wind lifted the capes of his greatcoat, and he glanced up to see puffy white clouds chasing across the pale winter sky. Like rabbits scurrying for cover, he thought, wondering if they marked a consequential change in the weather.

But Jane Ryder, bundled in her heavy woolen cloak, did not appear concerned. She sat perfectly at ease in front of him, studying the map and apparently oblivious of his arms wrapped around her, or his thighs rubbing against hers in rhythm with the horse's gait.

He had been decidedly aware of her, though, since tossing her onto the saddle and mounting behind her. Of course, he'd not been this close to a woman in more than a year, which doubtless explained why all the blood in his body was uncomfortably lodged where it ought not to be.

She gave no sign of noticing, but how could she fail to? On the other hand, what did he expect her to say? "Lord Fallon, I cannot help but perceive that you are exhibiting unmistakable symptoms of lust."

"There!" She pointed straight ahead. "Just over that next hill, I believe. Either that or we made a wrong turn early on."

"More than likely we did. Wilkens must have assumed

I would recognize the landmarks he sketched, but after twenty years, I remember very little about the estate. Shall we return to the inn and try again tomorrow, with a better map?"

"I suppose so. But *after* we've checked out the hill directly ahead, please. Should the house be only a few yards away, we really ought to have a look at it while we are here."

"As you wish, madam." If an accident and a long tramp through the snow had failed to slow her down, how could he call a halt on the lame excuse of a few clouds and a freshening wind?

As she had predicted, the next hill was indeed the one that overlooked Wolvercote Manor. He reined to a stop and gazed down at the house where he'd been born.

It was much as he remembered—enormous, impressive, and incredibly ugly. A patchwork mansion, assembled in bits and pieces over the centuries, it staggered across the landscape in drunken decay.

At the far left, from his perspective, were the remains of a fallen-in Norman castle. Most of the stones had been used to construct the medieval manor alongside, which melted into a rambling Elizabethan wing. Attached to that was a huge Bathstone block with wide marble stairs mounting to the elaborate entrance doors. Successive marquesses had added more rooms, always working left to right, and the result was a sprawling maze without a center.

Like the Fallons themselves, he thought—reeling carelessly through history, never looking back or ahead. After seven and a half centuries, since the Conqueror awarded this large tract of land and an earl's belt to a minor lordling who had saved his life, the family legacy had dwindled to this—a moldering manor house and a damnably reluctant heir.

He had understood what awaited him for as long as he could remember. No one told him. No one spoke to him at all when he was a child. His mother had died, his father ignored him, and the indifferent servants came and went. But he knew, and prepared himself. He set his goal right up next to the North Star, where he could see it in his imagination when he looked skyward at night.

Then, of course, he took himself to India, where he hadn't time to look anywhere but straight ahead.

If the magic of his dream had dissipated, his commitment remained unaltered. It gave him a future to reach for and something of value to care about. Now everything he had worked for lay within his grasp. Wolvercote was spread out before him, waiting to be reborn.

He wanted suddenly to turn away. A cold sensation crept up his spine. Once he set foot in that house, he would be enslaved beyond redemption. Or perhaps he already was.

Jane Ryder had been silent all this while, as if sensing his need for reflection. She would make the ideal traveling companion, he thought, were she not so disturbingly female. He urged Scorpio down the hill and made a hurry of dismounting.

Miss Ryder swung her leg over the saddle and slid to the ground before he could assist her. "While you unlock the door," she said a trifle breathlessly, "I'll find a place out of the wind to tether the horse."

"Fine." He untied the saddle pack, which contained the candles and tinderbox they would need, and located the heavy ring of keys his solicitor had provided. "We'll not stay long."

By the time she returned, he had lit a pair of wall sconces in the foyer and prepared a brace of candles for each of them to carry. Strangely he had felt nothing when he came through the door. Wolvercote was only a big, dark, ugly house, no more a home to him now than it had ever been.

Demolishing it would be a pleasure.

Jane Ryder tossed back the hood of her cloak. "My heavens," she said, brushing cobwebs aside as she made a circuit of the entrance hall. "Half the spiders in England must have taken up residence here."

"Not to mention rats, mice, termites, and, quite possibly, bats." He grinned at her startled reaction. "Far better company than my father used to keep, I assure you. But I expect you know more about him than I do."

"Possibly. Do you wish to leave now, or shall we go exploring?"

"We might as well make a quick round of the rooms that were in use the last few years. There aren't many, I understand, and all are in the west wing."

He led her along a dim passageway that put him in mind of an underground tunnel. It used to be lined with portraits, he remembered, but most had been stripped from the water-streaked walls. Probably his father had sold them, although why anyone would pay for the likeness of a Fallon defied explanation.

For the next half hour, they wandered through a succession of filthy rooms, stirring up clouds of dust and sending rodents and insects scampering for cover. Miss Ryder, her face and hair glowing in the candlelight, was a silent, comforting presence at his side.

In one large room where the windows had been boarded over, he recognized the heavy canopied bed that once stood in the master's bedchamber. His father must have decided to move downstairs, closer to his precious gaming room.

Nothing had been disturbed. The mahogany wardrobe was crammed with dusty clothing, and the drawers of a standing chest held stockings, cravats, and nightshirts. In the dressing room, shaving gear and brushes were spread out on a table.

He ought to feel something, gazing at the last few things his father had touched. Some sense of loss or regret, perhaps, or even the contempt he'd once held for the man who preferred dice and cards to his family. But this was a stranger's room, the death chamber of a diseased old man. It meant nothing whatever to him now.

"Some things are better forgot," he said, striding quickly to the door. When Miss Ryder caught up with him, he led her to the end of the passageway and stopped before a pair of carved walnut doors. They shrieked on rusted hinges as he pushed them open.

Inside, a large round table covered with green baize dominated the room. Smaller tables were set against the walls, and a roulette wheel had been shoved into a corner. It was filled with moldy cigar butts.

"The gaming room," he told her. "When the marquess was no longer welcomed at the London clubs, he created his own idea of heaven at Wolvercote."

She crossed to the round table and sifted through a deck of dusty playing cards. "There is a chapter of *Scandal-broth* devoted to Fallon's Hell," she said softly. "There was nothing of heaven about it. Fortunes were lost here. Two men put bullets to their heads after gaming away their inheritances in this room. In the early years, women were brought from London to entertain the guests. They were known as Fallon's Fillies, I believe."

"You *do* know more than I!" he said with a grim laugh. "The licentious house parties had not begun when I set out for India, although there was plenty of gaming at Wolvercote on the rare occasions the marquess was in residence. My own room was just over this one, and I rarely got any sleep when the punters were in full cry."

She gave him a curious look. "Do you game, too, my lord?"

"A fair question, given my ancestry, but no. Not on games of chance, at any rate, although there are many other ways to gamble. I did not earn my fortune by being cautious, Miss Ryder, but you may be sure I will never throw money away on the turn of a card."

"I am glad to hear it." She pulled off her gloves and tossed the edges of her red cloak over her shoulders. Then she selected three cards from the deck and spread them on the table. "Come look, my lord. Two aces and the queen of spades."

He went to her side. "Do you mean to play a game with me, Miss Ryder?"

"If you like. I shall turn the cards over and shuffle them about. Then you must locate the queen. Care to try?"

He studied her expression, which was absolutely guileless. Suspiciously guileless. "What are the stakes?"

"Oh, a shilling, I think. That's all I can afford. And since I am terribly clever with cards, you may have three chances to find the queen. To be sure, you are also clever, and may well beat me straightaway." She smiled, a dimple flashing in her cheek. "Shall we have a go at it?"

He nodded, rather certain he was about to be diddled.

She set down the deck she'd been holding, flipped the two aces and the queen facedown on the table, and began to move them about in a swift, fluid motion. Now and again she turned over the queen so that he could see where it was. He followed its path intently, convinced he knew its location when Jane finally lifted her hands. "Choose, my lord."

Three cards lay on the table, the queen in the center. With a smug smile, he turned it over.

"Ace of clubs!" Jane crowed. "But you have two more chances and know to pay better attention now. I'm sure you'll go right this time." After another series of lightning-quick moves, she again stood back and watched him select a card.

He slapped the ace of diamonds on the table with a growl.

"Oh dear," she murmured. "I thought for sure you'd found me out by now. Well, this is your last chance, Lord Fallon."

Again her smooth, long-fingered hands moved gracefully over the table as she lifted and dropped the three cards. As always, she showed him the queen on several occasions, and he followed her every move with keen regard. When she stepped back to let him choose, he would have bet Wolvercote and every penny he owned that he could pick the queen of spades.

The card he turned over was the queen of hearts.

Stunned, he stared at it for a long time. Then he glared at Jane Ryder, who looked just as smug as he had felt only minutes ago. "You *cheated* me, you infernal witch! Where the devil is the queen of spades?"

"Oh, I palmed it, of course." She raised a hand to expose the card. She lifted her other hand, which held the ace of hearts. "First two tries, you were bound to uncover an ace. I gambled that you'd not remember precisely which aces we were playing with. The queen of spades left the table each time, about when you had made up your mind where she was. I substituted the extra ace twice, and the queen of hearts on your third try, for effect. I knew you'd go for her."

"Devil it! I've never known what to make of you, Miss Ryder, but not once did I guess you were a bloody card sharp!" He felt heat rise to his ears. "Pardon my language. But then, I imagine you've heard worse. Did you make a living at this game before settling in to write a scandalous book with Lady Swann?"

She shuffled the five cards she'd been using into the deck and set it neatly on the table. "As it happens, a twelve-year-old boy taught me this trick. He made his living on the streets, and we chanced to share quarters for a few months. Since then I've kept in practice for the fun of it, but you are the only person I've actually played with." She cocked her head. "I'm rather good, don't you think?"

From the shattered remnants of his pride, he produced a noncommittal grunt. Then, feeling surly and embarrassed, he stalked to the cabinets lining the room and flung open the doors. When a mouse jumped out at him, fleeing in terror, he let out a squawk of his own. Pretty soon he was opening drawers and cupboards with a vengeance.

"I should have remembered," she said amiably, "that men cannot bear to lose."

He slammed a cabinet door so hard it wrenched loose from its hinges. "I am angry with myself," he said between clenched teeth.

"For choosing the wrong card? Or because a female got the better of you?"

"Neither. I had thought this house meant nothing to me, but clearly it has put me on edge." Turning, he held out his arms in a gesture of apology. "I'm acting like an a—like the backside of a mule," he corrected swiftly, glad to note that she was smiling at him. "Would you believe I am rarely out of temper?"

"No," she replied, her smile widening. "You seem to me an uncommonly temperamental man. If I had to guess, I'd say that you imagine yourself what you want to be, and undertake to ignore what you really are. But my opinion of your character is worth even less than the shilling you owe me, sir. I've little experience dealing with aristocrats." She regarded him speculatively. "Have I offended you?"

"Not in the least." He turned away and delved into the next cupboard. This time he hit upon something worth finding—several bottles of vintage wine and French brandy. His father always boasted of his excellent cellar, he recalled, although at the time he had no idea what that meant. He selected two bottles of brandy and two more of port wine, cradling them in his arms.

"We'll enjoy these over dinner tonight," he explained when she raised an eyebrow. "Better fare than the Black Dove can provide, I'd wager."

"This room has an unwholesome effect on you," she said after a moment. "Perhaps we should leave it."

He nodded. Since stepping inside, he had placed a bet on cards for the first time in his life and practically lunged for a few bottles of spirits. Were he a fanciful man, he'd imagine himself possessed by his father's ghost. As if to prove otherwise, he deliberately abandoned the port and took only one bottle of brandy into the passageway.

They ventured into a few more rooms, finally locating one that might have served as someone's office. Miss Ryder went immediately to the shelves and pulled down a heavy ledger.

"Shall I see what is here, my lord, while you go off on your own for a bit?"

How did she know he wished to be alone? With a bow, he returned to the passageway and set the brandy on the floor. Then he headed back in the direction of the gaming room. Close by was an inconspicuous door that opened to the servants' stairs. He'd used them often enough as a boy, mostly to sneak in and out of the house when he was supposedly confined to his room.

The narrow staircase was pitch dark. Lifting the brace of candles, he began the ascent, noting that the ceiling seemed to be a good deal lower than he remembered. Of course, he was over six feet tall now and had last mounted these stairs before his voice changed. Still, more than any other place in the house, this musty staircase held memories. Once he'd made the trip stark naked after someone made off with his clothes while he was swimming in the river. Another time he was smuggling a stray dog into his room.

Nearing the top of the stairs, he began to move swiftly, suddenly eager to see his small bedchamber again. Then he heard wood splinter as his left foot hit a stair and broke through. Automatically he flung his arms against the walls on either side to catch himself, but it was too late. His leg plowed through the rotted wood.

A spur of wood had caught in his thigh. Struggling to keep his balance, he tried to pull loose without doing any more damage. But it knifed deeper when he moved, and the jolt of pain sent him toppling backward.

He had a brief moment to be glad his leg had come free, and then he was bouncing uncontrollably down the long staircase. His head hit the passageway floor with a loud thump.

He could not have been unconscious very long. The brace of candles had beat him down the stairs by inches, and one candle still burned, so close to his head that it singed his hair. He batted it away and the flame went out.

He lay curled in the dark passageway, taking stock of his injuries. Pain raked along his left thigh, and assorted parts of him would be black-and-blue on the morrow, but he'd been damnably lucky. Nothing seemed to be broken.

Reassured, he attempted to stand and fell back with a groan. No wonder he had always hated this house, he thought dizzily. It had a malicious will of its own, did Wolvercote.

Chapter 7

Jane closed the ledger, sending up a cloud of dust, and returned it to the shelf. It contained nothing of interest—only a disorganized listing of estate purchases and expenditures from three decades ago. She expected the other volumes were equally useless, but carried a second to the desk for inspection.

Something, perhaps the noises of the creaky old house, seemed different now. Louder, perhaps, or more ominous. She paused beside her chair to listen. The windows were rattling, she decided, the sound muffled by the heavy curtains. Crossing the room, she lifted a swath of faded blue velvet and looked outside.

"Oh, my word!"

Snatching the candlebrace, she darted into the passageway, wondering which direction Fallon had taken. She was speeding toward the main entrance when a loud thumping noise caused her to retrace her steps.

Beyond the dim circle of light cast by her candles, the passageway was black as a cave. "Where are you?" she called.

Silence. Then, "G-gaming room."

When she found him, Lord Fallon was leaning against the wall near an open door, his greatcoat tangled around his shoulders. "I fell down the stairs," he mumbled. "C-clumsy oaf."

"Oh, dear." She came closer, lifting the candleholder, and saw blood dripping from a cut on his forehead. "Perhaps you had better sit down."

"No. Took me forever to stand up. Just give me a moment. Hit m'head. I'm a t-trifle woozy."

"Take your time, my lord," she said, her mind racing. How badly was he hurt? Ought they return to the inn or wait here until the storm passed? That might be only a matter of hours, but it could also be several days.

If only the light were better. In the shadows Fallon looked on the verge of collapse. Then, as if to prove otherwise, he lifted himself from the wall.

"Is it only my head ringing," he asked, "or is the house about to collapse around our ears?"

She released the breath she'd been holding. He sounded himself again, forceful and impatient. "A storm has blown in, I'm afraid. It has begun to snow, and—"

"Then we'd better get going. Will you bring around the horse? I don't know where you put him." He took a few steps, favoring his left leg. "Go on ahead. I'll meet you at the entrance."

When she reached the door and stepped outside, she was nearly toppled by the force of the wind. It screamed past her ears and set her cloak flying behind her like wings.

Fallon would change his mind about leaving, she was certain as she made her way toward the alcove where she'd tethered the horse. The enormous bay stomped his hooves against the cold, whinnying as she drew near. "Sorry," she told him. "The best I can do is take you inside, horse."

Clutching the reins, she led him to the front of the house. Gusts of winds had all but demolished the footprints she'd left only moments ago, and the tracks from the Black Dove Inn would be obliterated by now. There was no choice but to remain at Wolvercote.

Fallon was waiting for her just inside the door, saddle pack in hand. "We're not staying here," he said. "The dower house is close by, and I'm reasonably sure I know the way."

She looked him over, head to foot. The cut on his forehead had stopped bleeding, but when he moved toward her, he was limping noticeably. "What's wrong with your leg?" she demanded.

"A flea bite. Nothing to worry about."

She lifted the fold of his greatcoat and gasped. From a point several inches above his knee all the way down to the top of his boot, his buckskin breeches were soaked with blood.

"That is no scratch, sir. Please tell me the truth. Are you fit to travel?"

"Absolutely. Let's make for the dower house before heavy snow sets in."

He sounded so sure of himself that she was almost convinced, until he required several attempts to mount the horse. But when he'd made it onto the saddle, he lifted her up with ease and settled her in front of him. "Hang on, Miss Ryder," he said into her ear. "We are looking for two elm trees that appear to be embracing. Grandmama called them The Lovers. They stand directly in front of the dower house."

Ice pellets spat at her face like grapeshot, effectively blinding her as the horse plodded ahead, probably sightless, too. She wondered if Lord Fallon could somehow see the unseen.

She could only hope his instincts were on target, for they seemed to be going in no particular direction. As the long minutes passed and the sky grew darker, she was fairly certain he had mistaken the way. Turning her head, she brought her lips close to his ear. "Are we lost?"

His arms tightened around her. "Somewhat. We're in the vicinity, I believe. Watch for the embracing trees or the outline of a building."

She tried holding her gloved hands over her eyes to block the wind-driven snow, peering out from the cracks between her fingers. Her vision was clearer now, although she couldn't see any great distance. They would have to run smack into the dower house before she'd know it was there.

Oddly, she wasn't the least bit afraid, even though they were in considerable danger unless they found shelter very soon. But when she had been in trouble before, she'd always had to face it alone. Now, atop this enormous horse with a pair of strong arms wrapped around her, she felt unaccountably secure. It seemed impossible that anything, even a violent storm, could get the better of Lord Fallon.

His arm lifted and he pointed to the left. "The Lovers! We're almost there."

She finally made out a pair of bare-branched elms, taller than the others and standing close together. By no stretch of the imagination did they appear to be embracing, and she was certain he had fixed upon the wrong pair of trees. But as they drew closer, she saw the outline of chimney pots and a high, sloping roof.

He had spotted them, too. Dismounting, he helped her down and grabbed the saddle pack, located the keys, and went to the tall iron-studded doors. They must have been unlocked, because he was back at her side within seconds. "Go inside," he shouted over the wind. "I'll take the horse to the stable."

Expecting another unholy wreck like Wolvercote, she was astonished to see a small neat entrance hall beyond the rough medieval doors. The marble floor had been swept not long ago, and only a little dust coated a pair of console tables set against the wall.

The house was bitterly cold, though, and only the barest trace of light filtered through the mullioned windows. Less than half an hour before nightfall, she calculated, heading in search of a room with a fireplace.

The first door she opened led to a large salon with furniture concealed under holland covers. Next came a dining room, cobwebs draping the long table and carved wooden chairs. It connected to a small bare room, and just beyond that was a cozy parlor. Both were meticulously clean.

The parlor held a pale blue Grecian couch with a high

72

sloping headrest at one end, two padded leather wing chairs, several small tables, and a few logs piled on the hearth. Without question, someone had used this room recently, and likely slept here, too. A number of neatly folded blankets were stacked in a corner.

She returned to the passageway and followed it to a large, spotless kitchen. Several pots, pans, and dishes were laid out on a pine worktable next to a pair of tin containers. One, nearly empty, held a handful of tea leaves, and the other was filled with stale crackers. She nibbled on one as she examined the larder, which was too dark for her to see more than the outlines of a few jars and packets. There was a fist-size lump wrapped in cheesecloth on the shelf, and a few potatoes and turnips were tucked in a burlap sack.

She returned to the entrance hall. Daylight had all but vanished, and Fallon was nowhere in sight. She wondered if she ought to go after him, but had no idea where the stable was located and reckoned she ought to be doing something useful.

Gathering her cloak about her, she headed upstairs. The rooms on the first floor were filthy, but she located a well-stocked linen closet and made several trips to the parlor with towels, sheets, blankets, and pillows. Whenever she spied a candle stub, she stuffed it in her pocket. She rummaged through the drawers in the bedrooms, pulling out anything that looked soft and clean enough to use for bandages.

On her last trip, barely able to see in the flagging light, she removed the down coverlet from a bed in the largest chamber and put it inside a truckle bed. The roped bed was far from heavy, but she kept stumbling over her cape as she backed down the stairs, towing it along with one hand and trying to lift her cloak with the other.

What the devil was she doing? Fallon wondered, arriving in the entrance hall to see Jane Ryder pulling on something that resembled a small coffin. He mounted the stairs to help her.

"What is this you've commandeered?" he asked as she moved aside to let him pick it up.

"A truckle bed." She looked him over. "You were gone rather a long time, sir. I was growing concerned."

"It was dark in the stable," he said, following her down the stairs. "But it's been in recent use, lucky for Scorpio. I found reasonably fresh hay and a small sack of oats."

She led him to a parlor where she apparently planned to make camp for the night. He saw enough blankets and pillows for five people, a pile of stubby candles on a side table, and his saddle pack.

"I trust you still have the tinderbox," she said briskly. "We must get a fire going before the light fails altogether. The kitchen first, I think."

"Yes, ma'am," he said, grabbing the box from the saddle pack. Colonel Wellesley used to give orders in precisely that tone.

While he built a fire in the enormous kitchen fireplace, Miss Ryder carried in several buckets of snow and filled the heavy cauldron suspended just over his head. She seemed to know what she was about, and he was hurting in too many places to question her. She brought in a candleholder, too, so he was able to find his way back to the parlor.

There, in the light of his single candle, he selected three small logs and finally managed to set them ablaze. Fumbling idiot, he thought, stretching his icy hands to the flames. There was a time when he could raise a fire with only his knife, a small piece of flint, and a few dry leaves.

It was the cold, he decided, and the snow. He was used to long hot days, not these paltry hours of northern winter daylight. He knew how to survive in torrential monsoon rains but had got himself lost in a minor snowstorm.

In spite of everything, he was beginning to enjoy himself.

When he arrived at Portsmouth ten weeks ago, he'd been sure his adventures had come to an end. And nearly every minute since had proven him right. His life had become a tedious round of solicitors, housing agents, tailors, butlers, valets, and courtesy calls to the barest of acquaintances.

This might be poor stuff, as adventures went, but he meant to make the most of it. If only the devil would stop pounding on his head with a hammer. His leg hurt, too, although for the past hour he had been pretending otherwise. He suspected that fairly soon he would be all but useless.

On that thought, he began to light a few of the candles Jane had gathered. He hauled the odd-looking couch closer to the fire, deciding that Jane could sleep there, and was looking around for something else to do when she appeared at the door.

"We'll soon run out of firewood," she said. "Have you any objection to breaking up a few pieces of furniture?"

"None whatever," he replied, wondering why he'd not thought of that.

"Dining-room chairs will be easiest, I believe. Shall we have at them?"

Together they bashed the chairs against the floor and carried armloads of wood into the parlor, stacking them alongside the hearth. All the while she kept glancing at him surreptitiously, looking out, he was sure, for signs of weakness. Naturally that made him all the more determined not to show any.

He thought he had been fairly convincing as he placed his last load of wood on the hearth and brushed his hands together. "What next, Miss Ryder?"

She regarded him from the parlor door, arms filled with splintered chair legs and backs. "I'll take these to the kitchen," she said. "By now I expect the water has come to a boil. While I prepare a basin, will you devise a way to tear that length of muslin into strips? It's the one there on the table, beside the towels."

He bent and drew a slender, long-bladed knife from

inside his riding boot. "This will slice through most anything. But why—?"

"Bandages," she said, her startled gaze fixed on the knife. "We've left your wounds untended overlong, I'm afraid, but it's so hard to decide what to do first in these circumstances. Carve a few strips of muslin, please. I've found a small sewing box with needles and thread, in the event stitches are required, but there were no scissors."

"Stitches!" When he shook his head, it felt as if a cannonball were rattling about in his skull. "That won't be necessary, I assure you."

"A bit squeamish?" she inquired pleasantly. "Well, we shall see, once the wound is cleaned. I shall require access to it, of course. While I am gone, my lord, pray remove your boots and trousers."

Chapter 8

Jane took her time in the kitchen, certain that Lord Fallon would not be pleased if she returned at an awkward moment.

On a tray she assembled slices of dried apples, the tin of crackers, and two potatoes. She decided to save the tea for breakfast and filled a pitcher with snow for drinking water, setting it on the hearth to melt. Then she washed a pair of pokers for roasting the potatoes and laid them beside the supper tray.

Next she gathered what she would need to tend the wound on his leg. A bit of soap, hardly more than a sliver, went onto a second tray, along with a large stack of white napkins she'd found in the dining-room sideboard.

She went into the pantry then, hoping to locate a bottle of cooking wine. An application of spirits helped to forestall putrefaction, she had been taught, as did a poultice of spider webs. There were plenty of those to be found, of course, but she was unready to apply spider webs to aristocratic Fallon flesh.

The kitchen was warm now, so she removed her cloak and draped it over a ladder-back chair. Had enough time gone by? She guessed it had been twenty minutes since she left him, but her reticule and watch were in the parlor, and the hands on the kitchen clock were fixed at half past eleven.

How long did it take a man to remove his trousers?

Surely he was done by now. She ladled steaming water

from the cauldron into two basins, placed them on her tray, and made her way to the closed parlor door. "May I enter, sir?" she called, putting the tray on the floor. After a moment she heard a surprisingly cheerful voice.

"Come, bright angel!"

Oh my, she thought, fearing he had gone unhinged from the blow on his head. With distinct reluctance, she opened the door.

Lord Fallon, a sheet wrapped around him toga fashion, reclined on the couch like a Roman god. Like Bacchus, to be more specific, for he was cradling a bottle to his chest. When she entered the room, he raised it in a toast. *"Ave, Caesar. Morituri te salutant!"*

"Oh, I doubt you will expire anytime soon, my lord. Did you smuggle that bottle from Wolvercote in your saddle pack?"

"Best idea I had all day. The *only* good idea, I daresay. It's brandy, by the way, and prime stuff."

With an act of will, she stopped herself from rushing across the room to seize it from his hand. If Lord Fallon chose to drink when he should not, who was she to object?

"I was just wishing that we had a bottle of spirits," she said, retrieving the tray. "How do you feel, sir?"

"Much better than before I got the cork out of this bottle. Come have a drink."

"Perhaps later, thank you."

He was no help whatever while she put down the tray, wrestled a heavy chair and a small table nearer the couch, and sat beside him.

He gazed at her seraphically. "Do you mean to scold me, Miss Ryder? I expect I deserve a rakedown on several counts, but will it keep until tomorrow?"

"Certainly. And the brandy will be useful while I clean your wound. May I have the bottle?"

He took another long draught and passed it over. "I rarely drink, you know. Plays havoc with a man's wits.

But those had already gone lacking, and I had a bit of trouble separating my leg from my breeches. Pieces of me and m'trousers were stuck together, and I figured something liquid would help get them apart. Worked better when I drank the brandy, though. Got so I didn't care, you see, so I ripped everything loose. Now I'm bare top to bottom—except for this sheet."

She couldn't help but smile at him as she set the bottle on the tray. She also knew better than to look too closely at the long, lean torso stretched out on the pale blue upholstery of the couch. Rather a lot of him was not concealed by that muslin sheet.

"May I?" she asked, gingerly lifting the sheet from his left leg and bunching it around the top of his thigh. The cuts were not deep, she saw immediately, but there were a great many splinters, and blood still oozed from the largest of them.

His boot had protected the lower part of his leg, and his knee had somehow escaped with only a few shallow scratches. It was his thigh had got the worst of it, but only the front, she discovered after running her fingers over the parts she could not see.

She decided to begin by washing his leg and placed a mound of towels underneath to support his knee and catch the water. Then she soaked a napkin in the hot water and began to dab gently at the cuts, starting with the shallow ones.

He held still, making no sound as she worked. Once she glanced up at his face. He was staring at the ceiling, jaw clenched. Very much a stoic, Lord Fallon.

Relieved that his injuries were not so serious as she had feared, she worked quickly and efficiently. She was not, however, quite so self-possessed as she was determined to appear. To her mortification, even to her shame, the splendid male body stretched out before her was a powerful distraction. From the very first time she saw him in Eudora's parlor, fully and elegantly dressed, he had rendered her breathless. Now her heart was jumping about in her chest like a mad March hare.

"Good news," she told him. "I'll not be taking any stitches. But there are a great many splinters embedded above your knee, and they must be extracted."

He leaned forward and examined his thigh. "I don't see anything."

"The overdose of brandy must have affected your vision, sir. Fortunately, I located tweezers in an upstairs drawer, else I'd have been forced to dig out the splinters with a fork."

"I'm going to hate this," Fallon muttered as she brought another brace of candles to the table for extra light and settled beside him again, tweezers in hand.

"Hold very still, please. This will hurt far more if you thrash about."

He made not the slightest move during the hour it required to pluck the remnants of the Wolvercote staircase from his leg. Sometimes she thought to make conversation, to distract him, but she couldn't think of anything to say.

After what felt an eternity, she held the candlebrace closer to his thigh, located a few tiny splinters she'd missed, and decided she had finally got them all. A good thing, too, because the muscles in her hand and arm were knotting up.

"Tell me you are done, Miss Ryder."

"Very nearly." She stood and picked up the tray. "Wait here while I fetch more water."

"Where would I go?" he called to her back.

She'd expected him to retrieve the brandy in her absence, but the bottle was where she had left it. He was sitting up against the bank of pillows, arms folded across his chest, looking thoroughly disgruntled.

After washing the leg again with warm soapy water and rinsing it carefully, she placed more towels under his knee and reached for the bottle. "This will not be pleasant, I'm afraid."

"A devilish waste of good brandy," he said, lifting his gaze to the ceiling. "Go ahead, Miss Ryder. But be a good girl and don't use the lot of—*bloody hell*!"

He shot upright, clutching at the edges of the couch with both hands as the brandy seared across his leg. Even Fallon's stoicism had its limits, she reflected as he swore long and loud in a language she failed to recognize.

Finally he subsided onto the pillows, glowering at her. "Next time, if you please, just shoot me."

"As you wish, sir." She removed the soaked towels and began wrapping strips of muslin loosely around his thigh. "Whoever has been staying here left behind a few provisions, and I've put together a light supper. We should do well enough until the storm blows through."

"How soon will that be?" he demanded. "Before morning?"

"Let us hope so. But in my experience, the weather pays little heed to wishes, even those of a marquess." Satisfied with the bandage, she rearranged the sheet to cover his leg and leaned forward to examine the small cut on his forehead. The blowing snow had cleaned it well enough, but she dabbed a little brandy over the scratch before he had time to object.

"Who employed you before Lady Swann?" he inquired acidly. "The Spanish Inquisition?"

"How did you guess?" She began to run her fingers through his thick hair in search of a scalp wound. "Oh, my word. Such a lump! But no bleeding, you will be pleased to hear, so I shall cease tormenting you. For the time being," she added in strictest honesty. "The bandage on your leg may have to be changed, and I'll reserve some of the brandy in case it is needed later. You may have the rest, I suppose, although a man with a head injury ought not to be drinking spirits."

"On the contrary, Torquemada. My head is bound to hurt anyway. I prefer to numb myself now and confront the consequences tomorrow, if you don't mind."

"How should I?" She piled brandy-soaked towels and

basins on the tray. "So long as you are sober when we set out for the inn, of course. I doubt I could heave your soused body onto the horse, Lord Fallon. At some point, you will have to fend for yourself."

Wretched, magnificent female, he thought as she left the room with a tray that ought to be too heavy for her. But she carried it with ease, the same way she had so handily dealt with every obstacle she'd faced since the curricle accident.

Where had she come from? And how had she got to be what she was? He had met a great many fascinating individuals over the years, but none had captured his interest quite so much as Miss Jane Ryder. Although she wasn't the least bit beautiful, he felt a strong attraction to her. If he had met her in India, he would certainly have tried to seduce her. Hell, he wanted to seduce her now.

She was a vast mystery to him, this slender, iron-willed female, and one he meant to solve before they parted.

He reached for the bottle of brandy, which she'd cleverly placed a few inches beyond his grasp as if to make him consider how badly he wanted it. Badly enough to swing his legs over the couch and bend double to get at it, he decided, groaning under his breath with every move.

Why the devil shouldn't he get drunk? He was in pain from head to toe, snowbound, virtually helpless, and frustrated past good sense. One hour at Wolvercote had set memories tumbling one over the other in his mind, none of them good. Ahead of him loomed the future he'd worked for twenty years to achieve, but now, contrarily, he found himself dreading it.

He settled back on the pillows, bottle in hand, staring at the fire. Not *very* drunk, he told himself. When it came time to mount his horse and find a way back to the Black Dove, Miss Ryder would not have reason to be disappointed in him.

She bustled in with another tray, a pair of fire pokers

precariously balanced atop it, and gave him a wide, dimpled smile that made his toes curl.

He had been mistaken. When Jane Ryder smiled, she was beautiful indeed.

"Dinner is served, m'lord." She set the tray on the hearth with a thump and dropped to her knees. "We shall begin our feast with slices of dried apples, accompanied by stale but reasonably tasty crackers. There are mugs of cool water, too, but I see that you prefer brandy. When you hear me muttering under my breath in the morning, be sure I am saying *I told you so.*"

He watched her thread two small, withered potatoes onto the pokers and prop them against the firedogs to roast. She had finally removed her bonnet, and tendrils of long brown hair had pulled loose from the tight knot just above her slender, rather elegant neck. They drifted over her cheeks as she leaned forward to add chair legs to the fire, and certain portions of his anatomy that hadn't hurt until this very moment began to throb.

He looked away, staring instead at a portrait on the wall that seemed vaguely familiar. Another ancestor, he supposed, one who met with his grandmother's approval. She had lived most of her life in the dower house, welcoming him to stay with her during school holidays. Grandmama must have died sometime after he went out to India, although no one had bothered to inform him. He wondered where she was buried.

"My lord?"

He looked up to see Jane holding out a small plate.

"The potatoes will take awhile to roast, I'm afraid. I should have got them started earlier, but I didn't think of it." She swept his discarded breeches from the floor and disappeared into the passageway before he could muster a response.

Bemused, he made quick work of the dried apples and crackers. They tasted wonderful, especially with the vintage brandy to wash them down. The smell of roasting

83

potatoes tickled at his nostrils, and he could hardly wait until they were done cooking.

Small pleasures were the best, he thought. What were grand dreams and lofty goals compared to the crackle of a potato skin over a fire and the dimpled smile of a remarkable female? And why had she made off with his pants, he wondered?

An hour later, after devouring all but a few of the crackers, most of the apples, and half of Jane's potato, he got his answer. When she had carried away the tray of dishes, she settled on a chair near the hearth, his wet, torn breeches in hand, and asked for the use of his knife.

He found it under a pillow, within easy reach as always, and passed it to her. "Take care. That's a Khyber knife, and it's extremely sharp. May I ask what you mean to do with it?"

"I've washed the blood from your trousers, sir, and now I shall cut away the shredded material and sew on a patch."

"Will you indeed?" He chuckled. "What would Lady Swann say, could she observe her precious Miss Ryder stitching away at my unmentionables?"

She cast him a provocative grin. "I expect she'd be vastly disappointed that I had nothing to do with removing them."

He broke out laughing. "I am shocked, Miss Ryder. *Shocked!*"

"No, Lord Fallon, you are foxed. And you'll be glad enough of your mended trousers when we return to the inn, although I should love to see the Wilkens's faces if you arrived wearing that sheet."

"I might just as well wear it back to London. When she hears of this, Lady Swann will blast the tale through every drawing room in the empire."

"You mean to tell her, then?" Jane carefully sliced away a section of buckskin and tossed it into the fire. "I certainly do not."

"No? Did she not send you to me for the express purpose of dredging up more Fallon scandals? This would certainly qualify, don't you think? But I presume your silence is meant to spare your own reputation, which is perfectly understandable."

He saw her shoulders square as she looked for a tense moment at the knife in her hand. Then, with a small sigh, she went back to cutting away bits of torn buckskin. "It would be, I suppose, had I a reputation to preserve. But my activities are of no significance to anyone, which is one advantage of being poor and obscure. That serves your own purposes as well, for the beau monde will not remark what you have done in company with a nobody."

She was perfectly right, of course. He could, without fear of reproach, seduce a score of lady's companions and servants. But it angered him to hear her speak of herself in such a way, as if she were of less value than a hothouse aristocrat. Indeed, the proper young Englishwomen he'd met in Calcutta and Bombay hadn't a cupful of wits among the lot of them, although he had scarcely given them a chance to prove otherwise. Bored with polite drawing-room conversation, he invariably bolted at the first opportunity.

"I do apologize for landing you in this fix," he said, "especially as it will have been for naught. You have seen that there is nothing of value to be found at Wolvercote, nothing to interest Lady Swann or convince her to strike my family from her book. I am surprised she set you to this task, when she must know that the Fallons would not trouble to record their sorry history."

"You did warn me," she reminded him.

"Even so, I alone am responsible for what has occurred. Should you be faced with unpleasant consequences as a result, I trust you will allow me to be of assistance."

"Oh, you've been a great help so far, my lord."

He was beginning to loathe the way she had of skewering him in that have-another-watercress-sandwich tone of voice. Jane Ryder wielded her stiletto tongue like a

Medici assassin. And she was directly on target, for he had used her badly.

"I nearly killed the both of us," he said stonily. "We should never have set out for Wolvercote so late in the day, or left it again when the storm blew up."

"Who is to say? Not that you asked my opinion, to be sure."

"Because I am used to a solitary life," he said after a moment. "I have the habit of taking rash decisions and plunging ahead with only myself to consider. I did not mean to slight you."

"I know." Smiling, she handed him the knife. "Our small adventure will soon pass, with neither of us the worse for it. But how will a man of your nature settle in London, I wonder, with all of Society watching your every move?"

"Quite easily, Miss Ryder. I have made up my mind to become the very model of a refined aristocrat, the same way I determined to amass a fortune in India. I did the one and I can do the other, even if Lady Swann chooses to pillory my family in her book. Failure is out of the question."

He stowed the knife under a pillow, cringing as he realized what he'd just said. A jackass brayed to better advantage.

Unfazed, Jane Ryder was leaning toward the firelight, attempting to thread a needle. "I expect Lady Swann finds you far more interesting than your family, sir. The Fallon scandals are general knowledge, but almost nothing is known of the heir who ran off to India and returned a nabob. You still have bargaining power, I believe. She may well cut the Fallons from *Scandalbroth*, or suppress the book entirely, if you permit her to tell your story to the world."

"Gossipy old shabrag that she is!" He took one last drink of brandy and set the bottle on the floor. Already his head was swimming, and most of his body felt numb. On the whole, he thought, numb was a far sight better than the alternative. "Lady Swann can go hang for all I care, Miss Ryder, but I am certainly in *your* debt. I've risked your life, endangered your reputation, and spoilt your Christmas. Will it help if I send you back to Lady Swann with an accounting of my years in India?"

"Not in the least. Eudo . . . Lady Swann will always stand my friend, I assure you. But if you wish to win her over on your own behalf, you can best help yourself by approaching her directly. She is exceptionally partial to handsome young men."

Jane Ryder thought him handsome? He found that offhanded compliment inordinately pleasing. "I've no objection if Lady Swann becomes the first to hear what will soon be common knowledge. But I'd much rather talk to you, Miss Ryder, if you care to listen."

"As you wish." She was fitting what looked like a folded napkin over the hole in his breeches. "But I should warn you that I remember everything I hear or read. If you chance to say something I ought not tell Lady Swann, make sure you let me know."

Chapter 9

Jane began to think Lord Fallon had drifted off to sleep. He was silent for a long time, and when she looked over at him, his eyes were closed.

Swallowing her disappointment, she dug her needle through the thick layers of napkin and buckskin. It was better that he sleep, of course, although she longed to hear of his adventures in India. What an interesting life he must have led.

Then he sat up, punched at the pillows, and reclined again with his bare arms crossed behind his head. "When I was fourteen," he said, "I ran away from home. More exactly, I was rusticated from Winchester and decided not to return home. The life of a seafaring man sounded vastly more exciting than anything else I could imagine, so I headed out for Portsmouth and talked my way onto a ship."

"Truly? The captain hired a boy of fourteen years without question?"

"Questions are rarely asked on a small-time trader like the *Petrel*, where half the crew is on the run from creditors or the constables. We sailed between England and the West Indies for a time, and then trolled the Mediterranean for several years. Eventually we took on a cargo bound for Madras, and when we docked, I jumped ship. There were fortunes to be made in India, or so I'd heard, although no one explained exactly how that was to be accomplished. I spent a long time wandering around, scrabbling for food and shelter and learning to speak Hindi and Arabic."

"That sounds perfectly awful," she said, transfixed. "But rather exciting, too."

"It was certainly *that*. The ladies I met very much later in Calcutta asked why I had failed to settle peacefully into one of the British enclaves. Gentlemen, even scruffy ones without two rupees to scratch together, were always welcome to shuffle papers for the East India Company. But I lack the temperament for a desk job, and clerks pocket wages, not fortunes. In any event, I celebrated my twentieth birthday in Madras by stealing a horse from a merchant who had let me sleep in his stable, and off I went."

"Shall I assume that particular detail is not for Lady Swann's ears?"

"You be the judge, Miss Ryder. I was desperate, and he was wealthy. Years later I did send payment, but cannot be certain he received it or knew what it was for." He gave her a disarming smile. "I neither confessed my crime nor signed my name."

"I expect that was wise," she said, altogether in sympathy with his decision. No stranger to desperation herself, she had filched more than one cheese pie from unwary street peddlers, putting money in church poor boxes when she came into funds again.

"If you are disconcerted that I stole a horse," he said, "you will not wish to hear what I was up to the next few years."

"Oh, but I do!" She nodded vigorously. "Believe me, sir, I would never sit judgment on you. I haven't the right."

"Is that because you are concealing a peccadillo or two of your own, Miss Ryder?" He sat straighter against the pillows. "It occurs to me that I am wasting a valuable opportunity here, relating my rather disreputable life story while you sit like a Buddha, revealing nothing of yourself. From here on out, I believe we should take turns, my stories in exchange for yours."

"Rubbish!" She drove the needle straight through buckskin and napkin, directly into her thumb. "Ouch! See what you made me do!" She sucked on her thumb, glaring at him.

"Not so easy, is it?" He glared right back. "I feel like a damn fool talking about myself and see no reason you should be let off the hook. I want to know all about you, Jane Ryder. We trade confidences, or I am done with my tale, which means you'll never know what happened when I was made a slave by an elderly maharaja and presented to his young wife as a gift." He waggled an eyebrow. "Your turn."

"Don't be absurd." She made a great pretense of sewing, although her stitches rarely found their mark. "My life story is tedious from beginning to end, sir. It would bore you to hear it, and I've no wish to revisit what is best forgot."

"If I failed to please the maharani," he continued blithely, "my throat would be slit by the chief eunuch of the harem. But if I *did* please her, the maharaja would disembowel me with his own *shamshir*."

She swiveled on her chair to look at him. He was grinning, the fiend, confident that he had her full attention. "Well, my lord, you obviously escaped intact. I suppose you stole another horse."

"I might have done, if not for the chains and the guards at every possible exit from the palace. But I'll tell you nothing more until you give over a few nuggets about yourself. I'm a tough negotiator, Miss Ryder. I acquired my fortune making deals with men who could snuff me out with a wave of their hands. You may as well give in. Where were you born? Tell me about your family."

"Please understand, Lord Fallon, that I cannot oblige you. Since the day we met, Lady Swann has attempted to pry from me the same information you are demanding. It has become something of a game between us. Do you see? It would be unfair to tell you what I will not tell her."

"I don't see why," he retorted. "For one thing, she won't know. And since you expect me to speak frankly, why can you not do the same?"

For a hundred million reasons, she thought, casting about for one he would accept. At bottom, though, it was her pride. Only her damnable pride prevented her from speaking of herself, even to Eudora.

She dropped her sewing onto her lap, gazing through the fire into her past. Before she knew it, she was speaking. And once she began, it wasn't so hard after all.

"My father, if he still lives, is a baronet with four other children born to his wife." She looked over at Fallon. "I was not."

He made a dismissive gesture.

She returned her gaze to the hearth. "Mama worked as a chambermaid, until it became obvious she was carrying his child. He never pretended otherwise, which he might have done. Instead, he settled her in a cottage at the farthest edge of his estate and saw to it we were provided for. There was a small village nearby, but none of the children would play with me. It was a long time before I understood why. I soon grew accustomed to solitude, though."

When had solitude become loneliness? she wondered of a sudden. Loneliness had crept up on her before she knew it was there. Until this very moment she had not recognized it, or the emptiness where her heart ought to be. She had become too adept at pushing away her feelings because they got in the way of daily survival.

By now, surely it was Fallon's turn to speak. But when he said nothing, she plunged ahead, finding unexpected relief in sharing her experiences with him.

"Later," she said, "Father allowed me to join his legitimate daughters for lessons with the governess. I must have done well, because she passed me on to the tutor who was instructing the boys in Latin, Greek, and mathematics. Naturally I came and went through the servants' door, by Lady Ryder's order. I must have been a great embarrassment to her. When the boys went off to school, my formal education ceased. And not long after, when my mother died, I was sent to act as companion to an elderly woman in Newcastle. I expect my father paid her to take me in."

She realized that her hands had begun to shake. "So you see, Lord Fallon, there is precious little of interest to speak of."

"On the contrary. How did you come from Northumberland to London? Above all, how in blazes did you wind up with a poison-tongued old bird like Eudora Swann?"

"I must concentrate on your trousers, sir. Pray tell me about India while I work."

"Unless I am very much mistaken, Miss Ryder, you are a prodigiously stubborn woman."

"I cannot deny it, sir." She measured a new length of thread. "You are very much mistaken."

With a hoot of laughter, he tossed a pillow in her direction. It sailed past harmlessly. "Oh, very well, you maddening creature. But I shall save my most provocative stories until you are more forthcoming with your own."

As he related one engrossing tale after another, she finished mending his breeches and then sat quietly with her hands folded, taking care not to distract him. It seemed to her that he'd spent most of his time getting into trouble and getting himself out again, and she wondered when he'd found a few spare hours to gather his considerable fortune.

Eventually his voice grew drowsy, and when he stopped in the middle of a sentence, she glanced over to see him smothering a yawn.

"I believe it is time we settle in for the night," she said, bringing him an armload of blankets and the discarded pillow. "How can I make you more comfortable?"

He flushed. "I—that is—perhaps a few moments of privacy."

"Oh. Certainly. I put up a screen and . . . the rest, in the small room behind that door. It will be cold in there. Do you require assistance, my lord?"

"I hardly think so." He swung his long legs to the floor and draped a blanket over his shoulders. "You sleep here on the couch, Miss Ryder. I'll use the truckle bed."

"Nonsense. You are far too large, sir. You would not fit."

With a shrug, he limped across the room while she arranged his patched breeches near the hearth to dry, lined the scratchy rope bed with sheets, and went off to bank the kitchen fire.

She would have to sleep in her long-sleeved woolen dress, Jane supposed, envying Fallon his toga. What would he think if she made herself equally comfortable for the night? He probably assumed her to be a trifle fast, if not worse, because she lived with Eudora and assisted with the writing of her scandalous book.

Not that his opinion of her virtue mattered in the slightest. Lord Fallon could not be attracted to the likes of Jane Ryder, and was in no condition to follow through if he were. All the same, she decided that one half-naked person in the room would be quite sufficient.

By the time she returned to the parlor, he was stretched out on the Grecian couch under a mound of blankets, fast asleep. Careful not to look at him too closely, she added wood to the fire, pulled the truckle bed closer to the hearth, and curled snugly inside.

The arduous day had worn her to a nub, but her mind swam with visions of the stories Fallon had told her. She twisted and turned in the narrow rope bed, imagining the bright colors and exotic scents of India and a young man riding off on his stolen horse to make his fortune.

Even as she willed herself to fall asleep, she felt more alert and fidgety than ever before in her life. All her senses had sprung alive. She smelled the burning oakwood and the faint odor of roasted potatoes. Gusts of wind whistled over the chimneys and shook the windows. The house creaked, and sometimes moaned eerily, as if ghosts were walking the stairs and passageways. The fire rustled like aspen leaves in an autumn wind. She could hear ashes sifting through the grate and the low drone of Fallon's even breathing.

At some point she must have dozed off, because when she came awake with a start, the parlor had gone cold. She clambered out of the truckle bed to build up the dying fire.

When flames were licking at a stack of chair legs, she added the last two logs and knelt back on her heels, watching sparks shoot up the chimney. Outside, the wind shrieked, buffeting the walls and window glass like fists. The storm had got worse, she thought, hoping it was more wind than snow. Otherwise, they could well be mired here for days.

She removed the few pins that had not fallen loose in the truckle bed and combed out her hair with her fingers, wondering if she minded very much if they *were* stranded awhile longer. Lord Fallon would be emphatically displeased, to be sure. He was not a man to suffer being prisoner to the weather with forbearance.

She looked over at him, unable to see his face over the pile of covers at his neck. She could just make out a thatch of dark tousled hair on the pillow and the fingers of one hand curled over the edge of the down coverlet.

For a restless man, he slept like the dead. She gazed at him for a long time, rather surprised that he never once moved. But then, he had drunk nearly half a bottle of brandy and been clobbered on the head besides. This might be a good time to check the bandage on his leg, she thought. Unconscious, Lord Fallon was not so much a threat to her peace of mind—what little remained of it. Most had fled hours ago, or perhaps before that. It had begun to slip away the first time she saw him.

On her knees she shuffled to the couch and folded back

the covers from where she expected to find his injured leg, starting from the bottom for safety's sake. Gradually she disclosed an inordinately large foot, a bare hairy shin, and finally the spot below his knee where the bandage commenced.

As she moved higher, peeling away the covers inch by inch, she was relieved to see no signs of bleeding. Only when she reached his thigh were there a few dark stains, but they were dry when she touched them lightly with her fingertips. Taking care not to disturb him, she lowered the blankets a bit at a time, draping the ends gently over his toes and the sole of his foot.

And then she felt his hand stroke down her head, tangling in her hair as he rubbed her nape.

"How am I doing, Miss Ryder?" he asked, sounding sleepily amused. One finger teased at the back of her left ear. "Are you here to nurse me, entertain me, or give me the last rites?"

"You require n-no such thing," she stammered, leaning into his hand when she knew that she ought to be moving speedily in the other direction. "I wished only to check your bandage for bleeding. There is none of any c-consequence."

"Your hair feels like silk," he said. "I thought it would. I'm glad you let it down tonight. It looks nearly golden in the firelight, with touches of copper. Come sit here beside me, so that I can make out what color it really is."

"Plain brown, sir, as you very well know. And if you will let go of it, I shall return to bed."

"But I don't want you to," he said, a wheedling tone in his husky voice.

She began to suspect it was the brandy talking now. Lord Fallon was not the wheedling type. He did release her hair, though, and she heard the rustle of sheets as he moved to the other side of the narrow couch.

"I've made you a spot, Miss Ryder. But if you don't come and hang on to me, I'm likely to topple over the edge, and hit my head again, and bleed massively from all my frightful wounds, and expire because you were too heartless to save me."

"Fustian!" Propping one hand on the couch, she levered herself upright and turned to face him. It was, she knew immediately, a mistake of the first order.

He was sitting up against the pillows, covers bunched around his waist, with only a fragment of sheet slicing across his chest to where he'd tied it at his shoulder. All the rest of his improvised toga was twisted somewhere out of sight.

Mesmerized, she gazed at the wiry hair curling around his flat nipples, and the bronzed chest and muscular arms, and when he took hold of her wrist and tugged her to sit by his waist, she could no more have done otherwise than fly to the moon.

Her bones turned to syrup as he drew her closer, one hand between her shoulder blades and the other coiled around her neck. His breath was warm against her cheek for the barest moment, and then his lips brushed over her temple, and her eyebrows, and her lashes, and finally, as she strained forward to meet him, they touched her lips.

She tasted brandy when he deepened the kiss, and an intoxicating flavor that belonged, she was sure, only to him. She was certain of nothing else, except a profound need to be closer still to the heat that radiated from his body. Mindlessly, she dissolved in his embrace and kissed him back.

And lost her heart.

A lifetime passed, or only a few moments. The next she knew, his arms had fallen away and she was sitting up again, looking into his eyes, bedazzled.

He lifted one hand and slowly rubbed his thumb over her swollen lips. "G'night, sweet angel," he murmured as his eyes drifted shut. His head dropped onto the pillow.

For a long time, she could not trust her limbs to move. Finally she struggled to her feet and raised the blankets over him, stealing one last look at his chest and the slope of his broad shoulders where they rose into his neck.

So incredibly beautiful, she thought. No man ought to be so beautiful as this.

How was any woman to resist him?

Chapter 10

Jane wandered into the drawing room, propped her elbows against the windowsill, and gazed out at the stormy morning. Snow was blowing almost sideways in the peltering winds, and she could barely glimpse the outline of the tall elm trees that stood near the front of the house.

She had been rattling about all morning, mostly in the kitchen, trying every which way to distract herself. But once the banked kitchen fire was stirred up and fueled, snow water set to boil, larder thoroughly explored, and dishes washed, there was little to do but think. And only one thing to think about.

The Kiss.

Rest had eluded her altogether when she returned to the truckle bed, and she had not stayed there very long. While Lord Fallon slept the sleep of a fallen angel, she spent the rest of the night sitting on the flagstone hearth with her arms wrapped around her knees, staring blankly at the dancing flames.

Now, after many hours reliving each wondrous moment in vivid detail, she was no closer than ever to consigning what happened last night to the back of her mind, where it surely belonged. The unprecedented experience of being held in a man's arms and opening her lips to his intimate exploration of her mouth had left her wondering who she was. *What* she was.

Even here in the icy drawing room, her flesh still felt

on fire. Never in her life had she been more aware of her lips and tongue, not to mention other sectors of her body that rarely called attention to themselves.

She looked no different, unfortunately. When she'd stood before the mirror in the vestibule to arrange her hair, the same plain, ordinary face gazed back at her. She thought her lips a bit fuller, swollen perhaps, and her eyes seemed brighter. But in her rumpled dress, hair wrenched into a practical knot behind her ears, she would scarcely draw a second glance, let alone inspire a man to kiss her again.

When Lord Fallon saw her in the cold light of day, he would doubtless wonder what had possessed him.

"*Here* you are," he said cheerfully from the doorway. "I was beginning to think you had run off with my horse."

She whipped around, nervously grasping a chunk of skirt in each hand. He was standing with one shoulder propped casually against the doorjamb, arms folded across his chest. And fully dressed, she was quick to note, except for his neckcloth. Her gaze was drawn to the large white patch that reached down from the top of his thigh and disappeared under his riding boot.

"G-good morning, sir," she said from a constricted throat. "I trust you slept well."

"Like a doorstop." His eyes lifted to the window. "I gather we'll not be traveling anytime soon."

His voice was so matter-of-fact that she began to relax a bit. Perhaps he had no recollection of what had passed between them. He had taken a hard blow to the head, after all, and followed up by drinking far too much brandy. Besides, what were a few kisses to a man like the dashing Lord Fallon? They would be hardly worth remembering, let alone mentioning.

She didn't know whether to be grateful, mortified, or downright offended.

He lifted himself from the doorjamb and crossed

the room with his usual aggressive stride. "Why have you gone mute as a boiled egg, Miss Ryder? If I kept you awake all night with my snoring, please accept my apologies."

"You did not snore," she assured him, determined to match his unexpectedly genial mood. "I was merely examining your leg for signs of bleeding. The bandages really ought to have been changed before you dressed."

"And so they were. I am perfectly capable of wrapping a bandage, you know. And you must have done a superb job of nursing, for the wound is practically healed."

"I am pleased to hear it," she said doubtfully. "You look very well indeed. How do you feel?"

"Splendid. I have suffered no ill effects from the fall, and you were mistaken about the consequences of a few tots of brandy. In fact, I never felt better in my life."

She regarded him sternly. "You are lying through your teeth, sir."

"Yes." He didn't blink an eye. "My dignity requires it. And a generous, understanding companion would pretend to believe me."

"I daresay. Next time, take care to be stranded with such a paragon." Moving past him to the door, she grinned at him over her shoulder. "Come along, Lord Fustian, and I shall fix you some breakfast."

He followed her to the kitchen and obediently sat on a bench by the trestle table while she brewed tea and added water to the simmering pot of oatmeal. Glue would be a more accurate name for it, she had discovered when she ate her own breakfast. The heavy clumps, tasteless without cream and sugar, had stuck in her throat with every bite.

To his credit, Fallon managed to swallow several spoonsful before pushing the bowl aside. "Perhaps we should save the oats for Scorpio," he said, holding out his cup for more tea. "I don't mean to complain, but is there nothing else to be had?"

She went to the larder and brought out several jars

topped with beeswax and cheesecloth, lining them up on the table and pointing to them one by one. "Pickled cabbage, peas, applesauce, applesauce, and peas. There are a few more potatoes and some turnips, and what appears to be salted meat. If the storm has not passed before nightfall, I shall make up a stew for our supper."

"Our Christmas Eve supper," he said, reaching for a jar of applesauce. "And no plum pudding or gingerbread men tomorrow, unless we arrive at the inn in time for the Wilkens's family dinner. Do you mind very much?"

"Not in the slightest." She watched him pry out the wax with his spoon and dig heartily into the applesauce. "Elaborate celebrations are well and good, but Christmas is more truly a feast of the heart."

Spoon raised halfway to his lips, he looked up at her with an arrested expression. "It ought to be, I suppose. But I have little experience in the matter. The day passed without notice in India, unless I chanced to be in Calcutta or Bombay, where my fellow expatriates attempted to re-create a winter celebration in the stifling heat. I rarely joined them."

He put down his spoon. "It just occurred to me, Miss Ryder, that the only Christmases I can remember were spent in this very house. Grandmama had little money to spare, but she always provided a lavish dinner for the servants. We sat down at table together, and there was an old Scottish stableman who played the bagpipes while she passed out the gifts. They were simple—handkerchiefs, perfumed soap, and the like—but carefully chosen. Each year I received a small box of tin soldiers and artillery to add to my private army. I spent the rest of the day moving them around the drawing-room carpet, making war on battalions of knives, forks, and spoons. Grandmama could only afford to provide the English troops."

He propped his elbows on the table, resting his chin atop his folded hands. "Lord, I haven't thought about all this for donkey's years. Where does the time go?"

Where indeed? Memories of Christmases past began to swim in her own mind as she picked up the jars and carried them back to the larder. She recalled standing in line with the servants on Boxing Day, and how her father looked at a point over her head when he handed her a shilling and an orange. Mama always received ten shillings and a small ham. Then they were shuttled out the back door because Lady Ryder thought it improper for them to stay for the party and the dancing.

That was the trouble with Christmas, she decided. One expected so very much from it, year after year, never mind the frequent disappointments. Still, there was always next time, another Christmas only twelve months away, and hope.

She wished Lord Fallon had kissed her on Christmas instead of two nights beforehand. The memory, which she knew would be precious to her all the days of her life, would have been even more special had his timing been a fraction better. But then, Eudora often said that memories are what a person makes them, never mind the facts. When she was a doddering old spinster, Jane Ryder would probably recollect that her first and only kiss happened precisely when it ought to have happened.

When she emerged from the larder, Fallon was, to her great surprise, washing up his own dishes. "What shall we do to pass the time?" he inquired, wiping his hands on a towel. "If we locate a deck of cards, perhaps you can teach me a few of your tricks."

"The one I showed you is the only trick I know," she said. "It requires a good deal of practice, and I doubt you have the patience to master such a useless skill. Perhaps we would do better to investigate the upstairs rooms while the daylight holds. And do keep an eye out for candles. We are running low."

For the next hour, they roamed through a series of bed-chambers and small sitting rooms, gathering candles and sifting through drawers and armoires. Jane soon came upon a tortoiseshell comb and tarnished silver-backed brush, both clogged with several years' worth of dust. Pleased, she left them on a console table, meaning to retrieve them later, clean them up, and restore some order to her hair.

His lordship lost interest in their scavenger hunt within the first few minutes. After that he trailed behind her with his arms clasped at his back, making a false show of gratification when she found a candle stub or exclaimed over a swatch of antique lace.

He perked up considerably when they opened the door to a small, neat room that held a narrow bed, a chest of drawers, a tall wardrobe, and a rocking horse. She knew from the expression on his face that this had been his room whenever he came to stay with his grandmother.

"Holy hell," he muttered under his breath, pointing to the rocking horse. "That's the first Scorpio. All my mounts since then, the ones I've kept for any length of time, have carried that name. Until this moment, I'd forgot why."

"A magnificent beast," she said, watching him run his fingers between the pointed ears and over the carved wooden mane. "Why did you call him Scorpio?"

"I don't recall," he said brusquely, moving away from the horse as if embarrassed to be caught petting a wooden toy. "It sounded dashing, I suppose."

Fallon pulled open a few drawers and looked into the wardrobe, all empty, before heading quickly to the passageway. With a small sigh, she followed him, sensing that he had been more affected by that room and the rocking horse than he was ready to admit.

"Shall we try the upper floor?" she suggested. "The staircase is in the other direction."

He turned, shrugging. "By all means, if you wish to examine the servants' quarters. We may as well. There's very little else for us to do."

Don't be sullen, she thought as he led her up the

narrow stairs. It would be a very long day indeed if Lord Fallon got the sulks.

Men generally imagined themselves logical and straight-forward, even when they were misbehaving in the manner of very small boys. She had always wondered at it. Not the misbehavior—females could be equally tempera-mental—but the fact that men were able to create such a false image of themselves and expect others to accept it.

To her mind, Lord Fallon was mercurial, moody, impatient, sometimes charming, always supremely self-confident, among other qualities she had no business considering. His physical presence, his—dare she even think it?—raw sexual attraction rendered her incapable of coherent thought, even when she wasn't looking at him. She tried not to.

But her gaze was constantly drawn to him as they wandered in and out of the tiny, nearly bare rooms where the servants had lived in his grandmother's time. She marked every gesture he made, every expression that crossed his face, and logged them in her memory. If a cat can look at a king, she thought, a common secretary can surely gaze upon the Marquess of Fallon.

A heavy door, the large key dangling from its lock, stood at the very end of the passageway. "The storage room," Fallon explained, wrestling with the rusty key. "Dank and filthy, I would expect."

It was certainly dark. When the door swung open, she saw one pale shaft of light wobbling in through the lone window, outlining a large number of trunks and boxes.

"How wonderful!" she exclaimed. "A treasure trove. Why don't you explore, sir, while I bring up some candles?"

Before he could object, she was speeding down the passage, rather expecting him to follow her. But when she looked back, he had disappeared into the room. And by the time she returned, a brace of candles in each hand, he was sitting cross-legged in front of an open cedar chest.

"Come see, Miss Ryder. I think these are some of my grandmother's ball gowns. They must date back half a century or more."

Jane set the candles on two nearby boxes and leaned over to peer into the chest, choking as the strong smell of camphor wafted back at her. He had removed a wrapping of tissue paper from a dress of pale blue brocade studded with beads and pearls.

At his direction, she lifted the gown and held it up to her shoulders. "It's incredibly heavy," she said. "However did she manage to dance, wearing all this?"

"Along with a tall powdered wig, I expect. But she had only one Season before her parents arranged a marriage to my grandfather. He soon whisked her off to Wolvercote and left her there while he returned to his usual rounds of drinking and gaming in London." Fallon's mouth tightened. "It was not a love match, you may be sure. Once he'd got an heir on her, they rarely saw each other. And when my father was old enough to be sent off to school, she moved into this house and lived here the rest of her life."

Jane folded the dress and placed it beside him on the floor. "I am sorry for it," she said. "She must have been very lonely."

"Believe me, she was as strong and willful as her husband was weak and dissipated. She ruled Wolvercote, for all practical purposes, and spent every penny of the money she inherited from her mother to improve the lot of the tenant farmers. Lady Swann would do far better to write about Grandmama than her repellent husband and son."

"Then tell me what you know of her," Jane urged. "It was precisely this sort of information Lady Swann was looking for when she sent me to you."

"Perhaps. But I trust that old busybody as far as I could throw an elephant." He dug into the chest, pulling out dresses and quilted petticoats, looking them over before tossing them into a pile on the floor. When Jane protested, he waved a careless hand. "They will be preserved, I promise you. I'll send people to see them cleaned and properly stored."

Hands itching to pack them neatly again, she followed him as he scooted over to a trunk and wrested it open. More dresses, less elaborate but still lovely with their hand-tooled lace and intricate embroidery, were chucked onto the pile.

"Ah. Here's something," he said, lifting a delicate length of cream-colored wool to the light. "A Kashmiri shawl. I used to trade in these. The finest, by legend if not always by fact, were so finely woven that they could be passed through a wedding ring."

He ran his fingers over the material. "Excellent quality. It's an *amilkar*, because of the embroidery. In the old days the shawls were plain, but the story has it that an artisan named Ala Baba could not wash out the tracks made by a chicken that walked over the material he had woven. He covered the tracks with patterns of colored thread and a whole new industry was born."

To Jane's astonishment, Lord Fallon put the shawl in her hands. "You must have this," he said. "I'll hear no objections. Consider it a Christmas gift, or a souvenir of your decidedly bizarre excursion to Wolvercote. Besides," he added softly, "Grandmama would have liked you enormously. I know she would be pleased for you to wear her shawl."

Choking on a boulder-size lump in her throat, Jane wrapped the soft wool around her shoulders. "It's lovely, sir. I shall treasure it always. Thank you."

"Well, then." Looking mightily pleased with himself, which made her want to laugh, he moved on to the next trunk. "What the deuce?" Frowning, he lifted out a pair of black-and-silver brocade knee breeches. Next came a frock coat to match and an elaborate lace jabot attached to a stiff collar.

"Your grandfather's?" she asked into the stunned silence.

"Possibly, although he was never permitted to set foot in the dower house. I can't imagine she would keep anything that belonged to him."

Jane heard a low rumble in his chest, followed by an explosion of laughter.

"By God," Fallon said when he could speak. "I'd wager dear old Grandmama took a lover! Good for her. I wonder who he was." He dug through the trunk, throwing out more coats and breeches and two pairs of high-heeled, silver-buckled shoes. Uncovering a voluminous opera cape of black satin lined with velvet, he stood and swung it over his shoulders, making her an elaborate leg and sweeping the cloak back with a dramatic flourish. "How do I look, Lady Ryder?"

She dipped into a profound curtsy. "La, sir, all England has never seen so gallant, handsome a gentleman as you."

"Or one in more need of a shave," he replied with a grin, removing the cape and folding it carefully. "I think I shall keep this, in memory of Grandmama's secret affair. Lord knows she deserved a better man than the one she was married to."

The notion of his grandmother frolicking in the dower house with a mysterious lover put Lord Fallon in an expansive mood. He rummaged through trunk after trunk, most filled with hand-embroidered linens and pillowcases, some holding fans, handkerchiefs, and knickknacks. Now and again he recognized something, like a porcelain shepherdess missing one arm that stood on the mantelpiece in his grandmother's room, and the ormolu clock he used to wind for her when he visited because the servants always forgot.

Jane sat on a box and watched him. He spoke to her, often using her name, but she suspected he was only dimly aware of her presence as he called up experiences from a past he had forgot until now.

His mother had died when he was five years old, Jane knew from Eudora's account. He was sent off to Winchester when he was eight. But for a little time, on school holidays, he stayed in this house with a grandmother who took the small boy to her heart. She gave him a rocking horse and tin soldiers. She put him in charge of her special ormolu clock, which the servants had doubtless tended perfectly well, to make him feel important.

Above all, she had loved him.

You are a rich marquess, she thought, gazing at his profile through watery eyes, *and I a nobody earning my living as best I can. But we have much in common, you and I, when all the money and social distinctions are peeled away.*

Thank the Lord he could not read her thoughts. He kept his emotions so strictly guarded that he would be revolted to think a virtual stranger was sitting a short distance away, analyzing him like a bug on a pin. She could never tell him that she knew how he felt, or that her heart ached for him when he lifted something he recognized and cradled it between his large hands.

He had become more careful now with the things he found, replacing them in the trunks or setting them gingerly aside. "Have you a hairpin?" he asked when he tried to open a small trunk that was apparently locked.

She passed one over, and in less than a minute he was raising the lid. Then he took out a small laquered box and set it on the floor. It, too, was locked, but not for long. Lord Fallon, she thought, could well have a rewarding career as a burglar. Or perhaps he'd already had one. Curious, she went to kneel beside him and saw an assortment of old jewelry in the lacquered box.

He raised an intricate filigree necklace to the light. "This was Grandmama's favorite. She always wore it when she dressed for dinner. I remember that cameo brooch, too. But there is nothing here of value, I'm afraid. My grandfather sold most of her jewelry to pay his gaming debts."

Jane picked up a painted miniature set in a gilt frame. "Is this a picture of your grandmother?"

"No. That was her mother, Lady Belva Urquhart. Grandmama kept this miniature on her bed table for inspiration, she told me. As I recall, Lady Belva shot her first husband between the eyes and went on to marry Lord Urquhart for his money. Grandmama was their only child." He raised a brow. "You've probably heard this story from Lady Swann."

"No. It happened before her time, I expect. But this is all far more interesting than the redundant tales in *Scandalbroth*. I am sure Lady Swann would love to know all the gory details of Lady Belva's story."

"Well, *I* don't know them." He replaced the jewelry case in the trunk and pulled out a square wooden box. "Grandmama said only that Lady Belva's first husband was a notorious brute and that his demise was generally regarded as a blessing. The case never came to trial."

As she watched, Lord Fallon opened the wooden box. "My God," he whispered. Hand shaking, he passed her a painted metal figure about four inches tall. "The Duke of Marlborough," he said. "Commander of my troops. They are all here. The entire army is here in this box. I cannot imagine why she kept them."

Jane examined the roughly carved figure of the Duke of Marlborough, paint peeling from his red coat, the tip of his sword broken off. "So that you could give them to your son, of course."

He looked up at her in surprise. "I mean to sire an heir, naturally. That is my first duty, once I've selected a wife. But do you know, until this moment I never once thought of the Fallon heir as a small boy. What the devil will I do with a son between the time he is born and the day he claims what I mean to build for him?"

Love him, Jane thought immediately. *Love him.*

"No matter," Fallon said, replacing the box of soldiers in the trunk. "He'll want a modern army, I expect, not these ancient fellows. And a mighty French army to battle, with Bonaparte leading the enemy charge."

"Yes." Jane pretended not to notice when Fallon slipped the Duke of Marlborough into his pocket. "I daresay you will buy him an expensive collection of infantry and cavalry and artillery. But these beat-up tin soldiers will always be his favorites, I promise you. He will play with them more than all the others, because they once belonged to his papa."

"Humbug." Fallon got to his feet and stalked to the tiny window, glancing back at her over his shoulder. "No Fallon with a grain of sense ever wished to be anything like his father—not that there has been a sensible Fallon male born in the last two centuries. I am as mad as all the others, you know."

Unsure how to respond to that startling declaration, she was casting about for a change of subject when he began rubbing his sleeve against the window.

"Salvation is at hand!" he announced, turning to her with an exuberant smile. "The wind is quieting, and I'm almost certain I saw a slice of blue sky. Let's go have a better look."

Jane blew out the candles, picked up the black cape, and hurried after him. When she arrived in the entrance hall, he was already outside, knee-deep in snow, gazing up at the sky.

"See there!" He pointed a finger. "A patch of blue. And there's another."

The wind did seem to have lessened fractionally, but any blue sky he may have spotted was covered with clouds again when she looked overhead. Nonetheless, to judge from the elated expression on his face, one would have thought summer had come roaring in.

He steamed past her into the house, grabbed his great-coat from the hook, and emerged with one arm stuffed into a sleeve. "I'm going out for a look around," he informed her, fumbling for the other sleeve. "Scorpio needs to be exercised. Don't worry. I'll be back before dark."

Before she could so much as wave farewell, he was on his way to the stable.

Chapter 11

As Lord Fallon disappeared around the side of the house, Jane looked up at the gray clouds scudding across the sky. They marked the end of the storm, she thought, or perhaps the beginning of a new one hard on its heels.

In any event, nightfall was little more than an hour away. Please heaven the hotheaded Lord Fallon knew what time it was and kept himself within quick reach of shelter. Sometimes he hadn't the sense God gave a parsnip.

It's Christmas Eve, she realized as she tramped back into the house and shook the snow from her half boots. While delving into the past with the marquess, she had forgot everything but him. But now she felt the spirit of this holy night wrap over her like the soft Kashmiri shawl.

Every Christmas he could remember was spent in this house. Could she give him another to remember? At the very least, she resolved to make their sparse Christmas Eve supper a festive occasion.

All fired up, she sped to the kitchen and began to assemble a stew of salted pork, potatoes, turnips, and peas. There would be pickled cabbage on the side, and hot applesauce with black currants for pudding. A careful search of the cupboards had disclosed the packet of hard dry currants, which were now soaking in a bowl of warm water. She had also uncovered small bags containing flour and salt.

When the heavy cast-iron stew pot was hung over the

fire, she mixed water into the flour, added a pinch of salt, and rolled out the sticky dough. Then she rubbed a small piece of salt pork she'd held back from the stew over a baking sheet, added rectangles of dough, and set the tray inside a brick oven built into the fireplace. Plain hardtack could scarcely taste worse than her gingerbread men, she told herself.

Nearly two hours had passed by the time she finished laying out the elegant dishes and silverware she'd found in the dining-room sideboard. A trip upstairs to the storage room produced a lace-edged linen tablecloth, napkins, and ribbons. She made up a centerpiece, too, of evergreen branches from a tree growing near the front door, red ribbons, and candles.

The kitchen was fragrant with the smell of simmering stew. She checked the hardtack, just starting to go brown, and took a few minutes to comb out her hair and tie it back with one of the ribbons.

Fallon would be chilled and hungry when he returned, she thought, crossing to the window and gazing out at the darkening sky. Visions of him wandering lost in the snowy woodlands or, worse, lying injured after a fall, chased through her imagination as another half hour passed with no sign of him.

She was pacing the kitchen, nibbling at a piece of cold tasteless hardtack, when she heard him come into the house. By now she was too annoyed to go out and meet him. The wretch could very well come and find her, and he'd better have a good explanation for worrying her half to death.

Moments later he burst into the kitchen, carrying a pair of storm lanterns, an exhilarated grin on his face. "Hullo, Miss Ryder. Is supper ready? I've got a wolf in my stomach."

She shook her head, all her anger evaporating like the steam that rose from his wet hair as he moved to the fire. Insufferable man. Lord Fallon had best select a wife with an inexhaustible store of patience, for she was certainly going to need it.

"I found a dozen of these in the stable," he said, setting the lanterns near the hearth. "They all have candles, and I'll bring them in if we start to run low. Or"—he gave her a sideways glance—"we can use them to find our way back to the inn tonight."

She dropped onto the bench with a thump. "You believe we ought to try?"

"The sky is clear, and there's no wind to speak of." He stripped off his gloves and coat, letting them fall to the floor, and held his hands to the fire. "If this is only a break in the storm, we should have a go at it while we can."

"Am I to understand you found the direction, sir?"

"Not . . . precisely. I got back to Wolvercote without difficulty, and from there tried several likely routes to the inn. But the snow has drifted considerably, altering the landscape beyond recognition."

"I wonder your horse did not stumble and bury the both of you," she said, pressing her hands together to keep them from shaking. One wrong turn, one misstep, and he could well have frozen to death out there.

"Scorpio did stumble," Fallon admitted, "although he managed to recover after I was tossed from the saddle. No harm done. It should be perfectly safe for us to travel if I walk ahead with a lantern, holding the reins and watching out for gullies and snowdrifts."

"You have made up your mind, then."

"Not at all. Naturally, were I on my own, I'd head out immediately. And if I had the slightest idea which way to go, I would do my best to convince you to come with me now. But the decision is wholly yours, Miss Ryder. Shall we risk getting lost in the dead of night, or wait until daylight in hopes the clear weather holds? You make the call."

"Oh, thank you very much, sir. What if I guess wrong?"

He shrugged. "We are tossing dice, and there is no way to reckon how they'll turn up. But as the Fallons are rarely in luck when they gamble, I prefer to leave the choice in your hands."

"I'll think it over while we have supper," she temporized, although she had already made up her mind. Never mind that he was itching to be on the move. That was his nature, and he would fret all night if the skies remained clear enough for them to travel. But yesterday's storm had blown in swiftly, and another could do the same. They would manage well enough here for the time being, although she wondered if it had been a mistake to cook up nearly all their meager provisions.

"You have gone to a great deal of trouble," he said, apparently noticing his surroundings for the first time.

"Not really. It's a special night, sir, and I was of a mood to celebrate."

"Well, so am I." He smiled. "But you must let me help. What shall I do?"

She briefly imagined him wreaking havoc in the kitchen and shook her head. "Perhaps it will be best if you keep out of my way for now."

"Yes, ma'am." He clicked his heels together and gave her a mocking salute before taking up a position in the corner with his back propped against the wall. "I am not altogether useless, you know," he said after a few moments. "At the very least, I am capable of lifting heavy objects."

"I shall keep that in mind," she assured him, dishing the pickled cabbage onto a pair of saucers and carrying them to the table. When she tried to turn around, he was directly behind her.

"What is *that* supposed to be?" he asked, pointing at the cabbage.

"Taste it and see, my lord." Slipping past him, she returned to the fire and stirred the stew with a long-handled spoon.

"That smells good," he said, leaning over her shoulder for a closer look. "What are those little green things?"

"Peas," she said between clenched teeth.

"I hate peas."

"Then you'll just have to pick them out of your dish, won't you?"

To her relief, he wandered back to the worktable. Was the man never still? She began to ladle the stew, peas and all, into a ceramic tureen.

"Umm," he said. "These raisins are good."

She glanced over her shoulder and saw him dipping his fingers into her precious store of currants.

"*Stop* that!" Bounding across the room, she slapped his hand away. Currants flew in every which direction. "See what you've done? Those were meant for the applesauce!"

"What's the difference if I eat them now or later?" he inquired, looking offended. "There's more than half of them left. You can put them all in your applesauce. I'll take mine plain."

Indeed you will, she thought crossly. "I was trying to create something of a Christmas pudding," she said. "But never mind. The stew is nearly ready to serve, so why don't you light the candles on the centerpiece and take your place at table?"

He brushed a finger, wet from the water in the bowl of currants, down her nose. "Am I getting on your nerves, Miss Ryder? Truly, I am sorry for oversetting you, especially after you have gone to so much trouble preparing this lovely Christmas feast."

It was a mistake to look into his eyes, she knew a fraction of a second after she'd done it. Torquemada himself would pardon this man for heresy, and likely propose him as a candidate for pope, were he to judge Lord Fallon's nature by those saintly amber eyes.

"I am impossible, you know," he said. "I don't mean to be, but I cannot seem to help it."

Oh dear. With all her might, she quelled a misbegotten urge to wrap her arms around him and confess that she would forgive him anything, anything at all. As if he really cared, she chided herself. When they had returned to London, there was little chance she would ever see him again.

"Do light the candles, sir," she said crisply, returning to the hearth. As she dished up the rest of the stew, she stole a glance at him.

Mouth set in a taut line, he was touching a kitchen candle to the tapers on the centerpiece. She thought he looked rather dejected, but that was probably a trick of the wavery light.

She was convinced of it when he smilingly took the tureen from her hands. Thank the Lord, she had not offended him. But truly, what was a servant to say when a marquess apologized for his behavior, especially when he'd done nothing more reprehensible than purloin a handful of currants?

And dear heavens, she'd had the audacity to slap his hand! Heat flooded her cheeks at the very thought of it. Worst of all, it had felt perfectly natural at the time, as if the two of them were longtime friends. Or more than friends.

He had kissed her, after all.

And she had slapped him.

It might make a hair of sense, she supposed, if she'd slapped him *because* he kissed her.

She carried the platter of hardtack to the table and sat across from him, waving her hand when he politely began to stand. He had already polished off a healthy portion of stew.

"I was famished," he said around a mouthful of pickled cabbage. "Sorry. I should have waited for you."

"Not at all." She unfolded her napkin and placed it on her lap. "But I believe we ought to say grace, my lord. This *is* Christmas Eve."

"Yes. Assuredly." He put down his fork. "Go ahead."

"Not I, sir. As the ranking person at this table, you must do it."

"Who the devil made *that* rule?" he objected with a scowl. "Besides, I don't know how."

"Then it is past time you learned," she replied, wondering why she persisted when it was of little consequence who offered the prayer. But she was curious to know what he would say to God if compelled to address Him, even under these contrived circumstances. "A simple expression of gratitude for salted pork and turnips will do, you know. Unless I am mistaken, the Lord is not particular about the words we say, so long as they come from the heart."

She folded her hands and bowed her head, watching him through her lashes. Following her example, he folded his hands and closed his eyes.

"Th-thank you, God," he said, stumbling over the words. "Thank you for leading us to this house through the storm, and stocking the kitchen so we'd have something to eat. And . . . ah, for Miss Ryder, who has been a trouper through it all. Take care she comes to no harm, will you? Oh, and it would help greatly if you could direct us back to the inn tomorrow. Otherwise, that's about it for now. Unless Miss Ryder has something to add."

When she looked up, he was gazing back with a disconcerted expression.

"Have you?" he asked. "Something to add?"

She lifted her water glass. "Only this. Happy birthday, Lord Jesus."

Fallon lifted his glass and clinked it against hers in a toast. "Do you know, Miss Ryder, that half the people on this earth have never even heard of Christmas? And many of those who have, like me, generally let the day go by like any other." His brow knitted in a puzzled frown. "But this afternoon, when I was riding alone through the

118

snowfields, I felt the air quivering as if in anticipation of some great event. Why is that?"

Why indeed? How she had longed for someone to talk with her about such things. The mysteries of the universe, yes, and why nations went to war, and how it was that innocent children suffered while villains prospered.

She set her glass on the table with a quivering hand. "I often wonder, too. In the end, I can only accept that God knows what He is about. Christmas is one of His special gifts, I think, but I'm sure He has other gifts for the people who know nothing of it, like the ones you met in India."

"Just so," he said, nodding. "One day, we shall speak of this again. I find myself strangely curious to know what you are thinking, Miss Ryder, about all manner of subjects. But for now, your supper is getting cold."

A comfortable silence fell over the table as they ate. The stew, Jane realized after a spoonful or two, was overly salty from the pork and otherwise devoid of flavor. The hardtack tasted exactly like what it was—baked flour and water. After one bite of pickled cabbage, she passed her dish to Lord Fallon, who made quick work of it.

All in all, she had never enjoyed a meal so much as this one. Which proved, she thought, that the company of a handsome man could spice up even the worst of dinners.

"Had I left you peacefully in London where you belong," Fallon said as he launched into his third helping of stew, "what would you be doing tonight?"

"Christmas services at Saint Martin-in-the-Fields, I suppose. I went there last year. The music was glorious. And you?"

"Working. Perhaps reading." He dunked a piece of hardtack into the gravy. "Certainly nothing I would enjoy nearly so much as sharing this supper with you."

"Nonsense." She knew she was blushing furiously.

"Lies drip from your tongue like honey, Lord Fallon. I expect you even taradiddled your way out of that predicament you never finished telling me about last night."

He raised a questioning brow.

"You remember," she said. "The one with the maharaja."

"What maharaja?"

"He was going to slit your throat if you failed to please his wife and disembowel you if you did."

"Ah." He propped his elbows on the table and rested his chin on his folded hands. "*That* maharaja."

Light dawned. "Oh, infamous!" She jabbed her spoon in his direction. "You made up that entire story? It's a wonder someone has not long since hung you up by your tongue, sir. But why would you tell me such a clanker?"

"To convince you to tell me about yourself, of course. You were making me do all the talking, until I cast out a bribe."

"You ought to be ashamed of yourself, horse-thieving currant filcher that you are. Was everything else you told me equally untrue?"

"Are you angry?" He regarded her uncertainly. "Much of last night is fairly hazy in my mind, to be sure, but I am generally honest."

"When it suits you," she fired back.

"Because I am a practical man, Miss Ryder. But all the same, I value integrity. I even aspire to it. Perhaps I should employ you as a reserve conscience, to set me back on the path of righteousness when my own conscience fails me."

"Given our sorry performance together thus far," she advised him scornfully, "we'll be lucky to find the path to the Black Dove Inn."

"You are mistaken. I am persuaded we make an excellent team. All the credit is yours, of course, but I am gradually learning the art of compromise. And sometimes," he added with a grin, "I can be positively obliging. For example, you will note that I have managed to choke down your detestable peas without a single complaint."

"You have managed, sir, to slip them into your napkin when you thought I wasn't looking."

Color flamed in his cheeks as he set the rolled-up napkin, green with mushed peas, on the table. "Does nothing escape your eyes, Miss Ryder?"

"I expect the applesauce is heated through by now," she said, rushing away from the table. *Again* she had made a cake of herself. Who was she to reprove Lord Fallon, even in jest?

In his presence she forgot who she was. She lost herself. It scared her, this unaccustomed failure to control her tongue, not to mention her feelings. Always she had made herself into what people expected her to be. Even with Eudora, who encouraged her to express her opinions openly, she maintained her self-control.

But not with Fallon. Not with him.

She knelt before the hearth, stirring the bubbling applesauce as if it were a witch's brew, wishing she could evaporate in the steam.

Two warm hands settled on her shoulders. "I think we must talk about what happened last night," he said quietly. "Ever since, you have been on knife-edge, and so have I."

She could not mistake his meaning. Letting go the spoon, she came to her feet and turned to face him. "You must think me exceedingly foolish," she said, determined to be sophisticated in spite of her quaking knees. "I refine too much over . . . well, over a matter of no consequence."

"I kissed you, and you kissed me back," he clarified.

"Y-yes. But you had drunk a good deal of brandy. And suffered a blow to the head."

"Not enough brandy to render me witless, my dear. And while I confess to a hellish headache, the fact remains that I knew exactly what I was doing. And so did you, once the initial shock had passed. Am I wrong?"

Despite her frantic prayer, the earth did not open and swallow her up. Unable to speak, she shook her head.

"I thought not," he said. "Well, I hoped not. The fact is, Miss Jane Ryder, I had been wondering how it would feel to kiss you since the afternoon I saw you sitting all prim and proper behind your desk in Lady Swann's parlor. I wanted to kiss you when you came to my house with that blackmailing letter. I wanted to kiss you when I tasted your burnt gingerbread biscuit. And on from there, when I met you in the snow outside the Black Dove Inn, and when you sat in front of me on my horse—"

He took a deep breath. "I never meant to offend you. But I had wanted, very much and for a long time, to kiss you. And last night, I did. I'll not apologize for that, but I wish you would explain why it has put such a distance between us. Please. I have been honest with you. Tell me why you shy away whenever we look at each other."

"Probably b-because no one has ever kissed me before," she murmured.

"I know." He lifted her chin with the back of his hand. "I could tell. I felt honored."

"I felt honored, too," she admitted. "At first. And a great many other things I had no right to feel. But if you want the truth, Lord Fallon, I shall give it to you."

Stepping beyond the reach of his hands, she studied the worn grooves in the graystone kitchen floor. "You tricked me into telling you what I've never told anyone, sir. My mother lay with Lord Ryder, for reasons she never explained to me, but that does not mean her daughter is easy prey for any man who thinks it perfectly acceptable to . . . to . . ." Her voice faded.

"Yes," he said after a moment. "I see now. Will you believe me if I tell you such a notion never entered my mind? Dear God, Jane, if children were judged only by their parents, there would be no hope whatever for me. As it is, I have a legion of flaws that owe nothing to my disreputable father. I am a man. I am drawn, quite irresistibly, to kiss lovely, intelligent, gallant women. Sometimes I do more than that, if they are willing. But I never imagined that you would give me more than a kiss. I may have wished it—hell, I'm wishing it right now. But even more, I want to wipe the fear from your eyes."

"I am not afraid of you," she said. "Never that. But other men have assumed certain things about me, and I did fear you had leapt to similar conclusions. I gave you reason enough last night, I suppose. It seems I am irresistibly drawn to kiss handsome, intelligent, gallant gentlemen."

"Shall we simply remember our kisses as the nicest part of our adventure together?" he asked softly. "I know we cannot be lovers, Jane Ryder, but can we not be friends? I have precious few of those, and none I value so much as you."

This once, she knew from the open pleading in his eyes, he was speaking the truth. When she offered her hand, he enveloped it in a warm, gentle grasp. "Friends," she said.

As if to seal the moment, bells began to ring in her head.

"What the devil is *that*?" he swore, rushing to the window and towing her with him. "Did you hear that bell?"

Before she could answer, it sounded again.

He flung open the kitchen door. "Where is it coming from? I can't tell."

Together they listened for several moments, but the ringing had ceased. Jane drew him back into the kitchen. "I expect there is a church not far away, pealing the bells for midnight services."

"Nonsense. There isn't a church within miles of the estate. I'm going to have a look around."

"I'll come with you, then." She went to the chair where she'd left the folded opera cape. "Wear this, my lord. It's very cold outside."

He swung it over his shoulders and was gone before

she could finish donning her gloves and cloak. With a sigh, she secured the clasp at her throat and followed him into the star-spun night.

Chapter 12

Jane followed Lord Fallon's footprints in the snow until she passed beyond the light from the kitchen window. Then, pausing in the quiet, trembling darkness, she drew in a breath of cold air and gazed up at the sky.

Directly overhead, a thin crescent moon nestled against Orion's sword. She picked out the constellations she recognized—Perseus and Aries, Pegasus and Gemini and Cassiopeia.

On the first Christmas, a special star had blazed through the night, guiding shepherds to the stable where Mary and Joseph watched over a newborn babe. It must have been a night very like this one, she thought, clear and peaceful and shimmering with hope.

Starshine glistened on the snow all around her, as if she were standing in a field of diamonds. She imagined angel song, and Glorias ringing in the air.

Ringing as that bell had rung . . . if they had really heard it.

She set off again, picking out Fallon's trail by starlight, humming a carol. "Loo-lee loo-lay, thou little tiny child—"

"Jane!" Fallon's shout pierced the silence. "This way. Hurry!"

Following the sound of his voice, she came over a rise and saw the outline of a low building. The stable, she guessed, wondering at a small circle of light directly in front of it. She recognized his tall figure nearby and rushed to join him. As she drew closer, she could make out a ring of candles set in the snow, and the mound of evergreen branches at its center.

Fallon came to meet her. "You will not believe this," he said, taking her hand and leading her to the circle of candles.

She gasped.

Atop the cradle of evergreen boughs was a willow basket. And inside the basket was a child.

Two mittened hands waved in the air. "Ga. Ga ga!"

"Oh, my word!" Jane quickly moved a few of the candles out of the way, pulled aside a homespun blanket, and lifted the babe in her arms.

Delighted, the infant pawed at her face. "Ga!" Wide eyes gazed up at her. "Ga ga ga!"

Jane looked to where Fallon had been, but he had disappeared. "Never mind him," she told the child, who gave her a happy grin in reply. "What a sweet thing you are, my darling. Wherever did you come from?"

"Goo ga."

"That far away? Well, you must be very tired indeed after such a journey." Still murmuring nonsense, smiling when the babe replied, she noted the clean muslin gown, the knitted mittens and booties, and the bonnet edged with simple lace. They bespoke loving care but little money to spend. The child's plump, rosy cheeks glowed with health.

Fallon emerged from behind the stable, frowning murderously. He paused a moment, looking over at her and the babe. Then, with obvious reluctance, he came to a point several arm-lengths away and planted his boots in the snow. "I . . . you . . ." He pointed to the babe. "Is it all right?"

She took a deep breath for patience. "If you are referring to the infant, yes. So far as I can tell, anyway. But we should take *it* inside, because *it* is undoubtedly cold."

His frown became a scowl. "Pardon me. Should I have said *he*, or *she*?"

Jane had no idea. But the look on Fallon's expressive

126

face had roused every protective instinct in her body. The child had been abandoned once, poor little mite, and his lordship was already thinking "it." She knew how casually an "it" was cast aside.

"We'll soon find out," she said with an apologetic smile. She'd have gone on her knees to placate him, if necessary, but soon realized that his thoughts were already elsewhere. He wanted only to know how the child got here in the first place. To his mind, the sudden appearance of a babe in the snow was a problem to be solved. And so it was, she supposed, when a hundred other problems were dealt with first. "Did you find anything?" she asked, feigning interest for his sake.

"Hoofprints, bootprints, and the tracks of what might be a sled. Something on runners, anyway. I can't tell how many people were here, but one set of prints is considerably smaller than the others. The one who stayed behind to ring the bell hasn't much of a start, so if I head out now, I should be able to run him down within the hour."

"Are you mad, sir? You cannot leave us here alone."

Fallon came a few steps closer, eyeing the babe warily. "I fail to see why not. The house is warm enough, and you are more than capable of dealing with any problems that may arise."

"Lord Fallon," she said firmly, "the very last thing that matters right now is finding the people who abandoned this child. You simply cannot go haring after them until we contrive some way to feed the poor thing. Infants require nourishment every few hours, you know."

"Do they? I have no acquaintance among the infantry, Miss Ryder, and can be of no help to you in these matters. As for nourishment, well, you have—" He made a sweeping gesture in the direction of her bosom. "That is, you are the one with the necessary . . . equipment."

"Breasts," she said, watching him turn several shades of crimson.

"Exactly. You were formed to give nourishment to a child."

"In general, yes. But apparently you are under some misapprehension about female plumbing. I am no expert in such matters, but I do know that females produce milk only when they give birth. 'Round about that time, in any case."

His brows shot up. "Are you certain? I mean, cows give milk every day. Or so I believe."

"I am not a cow," she said in measured tones. "Humans are different."

"Do you know that from experience?" he demanded. "Have you ever tried?"

"Good heavens, sir! If you must know, to date I've not put my ability to suckle a babe to the test. But what is that to the point? You may be sure I would gladly feed this child from my own body, if I could. But I cannot. You must trust me on that point."

He pointed to the child. "It thinks you can."

She glanced down to see tiny pink lips moving over her cloak, probing for her nipples. The artless gesture, the incredible intimacy of it, sent fire and longing directly to her heart.

" 'Tis a purely instinctive reaction, my lord. I wish it were otherwise. But we both need you now, the babe and I, so please do not think of leaving us." She gave him a pleading smile. "May we at least go inside where it is warm to discuss this further?"

She could all but hear his teeth grinding. His own instincts drove him to the chase, she knew, as surely as the babe knew where to look for its supper.

He surprised her with a bow of acquiescence. "Very well, madam, we shall do as you say. Go ahead of me, if you please, while I make sure the blackguards didn't make off with my horse."

"Fine," she said, suppressing her relief. "When you are done, please gather the basket and candles and bring them with you." Without a backward look, she made her way to the house.

Arriving in the parlor, Jane went to the hearth and sat

cross-legged with the babe on her lap while she removed her gloves and held her hands to the fire. Two wide blue eyes gazed up at her with what she imagined to be absolute trust. For a moment they looked almost amber, like Fallon's eyes, but it could only be a reflection from the firelight.

When her hands were warm, she rubbed the babe's cold pink cheeks with her thumbs. In response, the infant gurgled blissfully.

What a happy little creature, Jane thought, and not in the least put out by these extraordinary events. When her thumb wandered close to the open mouth, it was immediately seized and vigorously sucked.

"I have no milk," she apologized. "Not there nor anywhere else, I'm afraid. Perhaps Lord Fallon will fetch you some from the inn." *If he can find it,* she added silently. No use worrying the child, who was listening attentively to her every word.

It seemed a very long time since Fallon had promised to join her. She refused to imagine he'd saddled his horse and gone after the . . . well, what *was* the opposite of "abductors"?

"Leavers"? What sort of people would bring an infant to this remote place, set out candles and lanterns, ring a bell, and scarper?

For that matter, how did they know someone was in earshot of the bell? It was sheerest accident that she and Fallon had taken refuge in the dower house. And no one lived close by. By his account, the entire Wolvercote estate had been deserted this past year or more.

Except, of course, for the individual who had recently slept in this very room and left jars of peas and applesauce in the larder. Perhaps she would find evidence the babe had been here, too, now that she knew to look for it.

Questions and questions and questions. Like Fallon, she found herself longing for answers, although milk and—fairly soon, she suspected—a change of nappies topped her list of priorities.

She heard the sound of a door opening and slamming shut, a loud thud, a blistering oath, and several more decidedly queer noises from the passageway. Moments later Fallon burst into the room, one arm wrapped around the basket and the other stretched out behind him, as if something were pulling on it.

Suddenly the *something* galloped past him and halted abruptly when he jerked on a short chain tether. It baaed a protest, digging at the carpet with its front hooves.

A goat! Glory be, a goat with a heavy udder, ripe for milking!

"It was tied up directly in front of Scorpio's stall," Fallon explained somewhat breathlessly.

"Oh, this is beyond perfect, sir. Did you find anything else?"

"That's all." He waved at the goat. "What more do you need?"

"Some way to actually feed the child, of course. We can't exactly hook the babe's mouth to a teat. Look through the basket, will you? Perhaps there's a bottle or a wineskin we can use."

He pulled a small handwoven blanket from the basket and shook it in the air. "Nothing more, not even a note to explain who the child is and why it—the child, I mean— was delivered into the care of strangers."

"Well, at least they also left the goat, which solves our most urgent problem. We shall improvise from here."

"No!"

Jane thought Fallon was addressing her, until she saw that the goat had seized a mouthful of his lordship's cape.

"Let go, you infernal beast!"

Goat and marquess launched into a fierce tug-of-war, with goat the most likely winner until Jane crossed the room to thwap it on the hindquarters. Thoroughly astonished, the goat released the cape to shake its head and glare at her.

"We'll deal with your megrims later," she said firmly. "And find you something better to eat than a musty old

130

cape." She turned to Fallon. "Do you know how to handle goats?"

"Obviously not." He removed his cloak and tossed it over the back of a chair. "Tell me what to do."

She smiled as the babe made another effort to locate her nipples. "This one is exceedingly hungry. Secure the goat in the kitchen, if you will. To something metal, because it will eat through most anything else. Then I'll do the milking, while you find a container of some sort for the feeding."

He frowned, nodded, and towed the recalcitrant goat back into the passageway. Jane heard a good deal of baaing, punctuated with a great many oaths, as the pair made their way toward the kitchen.

"Oh, dear," she said. "What a peculiar Christmas this has turned out to be."

The babe cooed in agreement.

Jane resettled the infant in the basket and found a spot where the fire was warm but not too hot. "Can you wait alone for a few minutes, while I arrange for milk and nappies?"

Two mittened hands waved back at her.

No wail of protest followed her departure, thank heavens, for she could not bear the thought of leaving the babe to cry alone. Dashing into the kitchen, she saw that Fallon had secured the goat's tether to the thick leg of a cast-iron plate warmer. He had also built up the fire, put snow in a kettle to melt, and set out a porcelain bowl to catch the milk.

When it came right down to it, she thought, Lord Fallon got things done. He had also disappeared, and she hoped he'd gone in search of a container for the milk.

The remains of their interrupted meal were strewn over the table, and the candles on the centerpiece had burned down to stubs. Was it only half an hour ago that she was sharing Christmas Eve supper with the Marquess of Fallon? Pledging her friendship as he had pledged his?

At the time, she had imagined that life could not get any stranger.

Kneeling beside the doe, she wiped the udder and teats with a wet napkin and placed the bowl in position. Goat was having none of it. She writhed against the tether, jumping about as if her hooves had gone on fire. The bowl went flying across the kitchen and shattered against the wall.

"*Bad* goat!" Jane located a metal pan to receive the milk and tried again, with similar results, although the pan remained intact when it was kicked away. She realized the doe was lunging toward the trestle table. "Smell food, do you? I wonder if you will care for Lord Fallon's discarded peas."

Apparently so. When a plate was set in front of her, the goat set to with a hearty appetite. Jane had served up everything but the currants before the doe permitted her to fill the pan with warm, steaming milk.

"Clever thing." She stroked the goat's head for a few seconds before coming to her feet. "You fuss until you get what you want."

"I hope you aren't speaking to me," Fallon said from the doorway.

Startled, Jane almost dropped the precious milk. "Certainly not. But I hope you've been as clever as this goat." She set the pan on the table and turned to face him.

With blatant pride, he held out the brandy bottle he had all but emptied the night before. From the grin on his face, she wondered if he had drunk the rest within the last few minutes. He beckoned her closer and dropped a small object in her hand. It was the cork, carved in the shape of a nipple, and he had poked a hole from top to bottom.

"Oh! This is capital."

"Not quite yet." He took it back. "Stinks of brandy, but hot water will take care of that." He rinsed the bottle with water from the kettle and dropped the cork into a cup of hot water to soak. "See if you can find a funnel."

She discovered one in the pantry and held it in place while he poured the milk. Then he retrieved the cork, inserted it tightly, and returned the bottle to Jane. "You'd better make sure this will draw."

She lifted the makeshift nipple to her mouth and sucked hard, dislodging a small chunk of broken cork that had blocked the way. Soon the creamy milk flowed easily into her mouth.

He laughed when she licked the overflow from her lips. "Do I get a pat on the head for being clever, Miss Ryder?"

If not for the hungry babe waiting in the next room, she'd have gladly stroked his head until dawn. Suddenly she wanted to touch everything that was alive and warm. The goat, yes, for it had been, at the last, a very good goat indeed. The infant, to be sure. And this resourceful man who kept finding, without meaning to, new ways to make her fall in love with him.

It was a night for dreams, she thought, but there was no time for dreaming.

"We have much more to do," she said, pointing to the goat. "She should be returned to the stable and tethered near a bed of straw. Provide her with hay and oats, too, for she cannot give milk if she doesn't eat. I shall feed the child, of course, unless you would prefer to do it."

He looked appalled at the notion.

"But first of all," she continued, thinking rapidly, "I expect you'd better pack fresh snow around the pan of milk and place it in the larder. I have no idea how frequently a goat can be milked. And there is still the matter of clean cloth for nappies. Cut rectangles about a foot long and a bit less wide. No, cut only one rectangle to begin with, until I determine the proper size."

Fallon saluted. "Yes, ma'am."

"Oh my." She felt heat rise to her cheeks. "Truly, I don't mean to be a managing female."

His smile was singularly sweet. "In this situation, Miss Ryder, a managing female is precisely what we require.

You see to the child and continue advising me how I can help. Short of changing the babe's undergarments, that is. I've no idea how it is done, nor do I care to find out."

Jane was holding the infant facedown across her lap, patting the tiny back, when Fallon returned from his chores. She glanced up when he came into the room, his arms wrapped around a bundle of white material.

"What in blazes are you doing to that poor child?" he demanded, eyebrows snapping together in a frown.

"Encouraging a burp, I hope. My experience with infants is virtually nonexistent, but I believe they swallow a good deal of air when they suckle and need help to expel it." She laughed. "Whatever did you *think* I was about?"

He dropped the pile of linens on the couch and pulled his knife from the ankle sheath. "Never mind. Any difficulty with the cork?"

"None whatever, sir. It was an inspired idea. The babe went at it as if feeding from a brandy bottle were an everyday occurrence."

"I am glad to hear it."

In fact, Jane thought, he looked inordinately pleased with himself as he sliced up a sheet and lifted a sample for her approval. It was greatly oversize, but he had yet to come close enough to the babe to realize how very small a bottom he was dealing with. "You might trim off a few inches," she suggested mildly.

"*Urp!*" said the babe.

"Oh, well done!" Jane approved, raising the infant and nuzzling the warm little face. "A most excellent burp, my love."

When she glanced at Fallon, he was standing with his knife dangling from one hand and a length of cloth from the other, gazing back with an arrested expression on his face. Then, as if embarrassed to be caught gawking, he went at the hapless diaper with his knife until he'd produced a reasonable facsimile of a rectangle.

And none too soon, Jane realized when the infant's face screwed into a look of intense concentration. Moments later a distinctive odor floated to her nostrils. The babe gave a happy gurgle of relief and gazed at her expectantly.

"Yes, I do see what you mean," she said. "Lord Fallon, will you fetch a basin of lukewarm water from the kitchen?"

He must have smelled the odor, too, because he shot away as if the devil were close on his heels.

Jane carried the babe to the Grecian couch and made a pallet of sheets to protect the upholstery before untying the soiled diaper. She was trying to figure out what to do with it when Fallon returned, maintaining a careful distance as he set the basin on the carpet and nudged it closer to her with his foot.

Dear heavens, she thought, tempted to chuck the smelly nappy into his hands just to see his reaction. She had not realized that men were so overnice about natural bodily functions. He withdrew immediately to the fireplace and rested his arm on the mantelpiece, whistling softly as he stared at the ceiling.

She deposited the befouled nappy on a folded sheet, cleaned the infant's bottom, and made fairly decent work of tying her first diaper. At the least, it did not fall off when she lifted the babe for inspection.

"Ga!" Blue eyes gazed at her with approval. "Ga ga ga ga!"

"Does it fit?" Fallon inquired, still examining the ceiling.

"I think so. She's a little girl, by the way."

His elbow dropped off the mantel. "I was afraid of that. Damn!"

Thunderstruck, Jane cradled the baby protectively in her arms. "Why so? What difference can her gender possibly make to *you*, sir?"

"None whatever," he said in a hushed tone. "But there are places—not England, I trust—where female infants are too often left by a roadside or in a trash heap to die.

135

The parents are desperately poor, and their reasons have been explained to me by people who are more in sympathy with their society and culture than I, but I could never accept any justification whatever for such atrocities."

Her blood ran cold imagining it. And he felt just as deeply, she knew. His face had gone nearly gray under his tan as he spoke, and when he was done, his lips were drawn into a taut line.

"This infant girl was well loved," she assured him. "The people who left her here took great care to be certain she was found and taken in."

"Good." He visibly relaxed. "For a moment I thought . . . but clearly I was wrong. She appears healthy enough, at any rate."

"Yes." On impulse Jane went to the fireplace and, before Fallon knew what she was about, lowered the infant into his arms. "Hold her, please, while I make a place for her to sleep. And be sure to support her head." When he gave her a stunned look, she arranged his hands and arms around the child. "That will do. She won't break, sir, nor will she explode. I have not handed you a wad of gunpowder."

"Ga!" the babe exclaimed, pleased with her new toy. As Jane watched, a wee mittened hand reached up and grappled Lord Fallon's nose.

Clearly dumbfounded, he gazed at the gleeful infant's face from crossed eyes.

Deciding that the child was in full control for now, Jane left Fallon to cope as best he could while she lined the basket with a sheet. Perversely she also carried the water basin and soiled nappy off to the kitchen, although the task could well have waited for later. She even considered washing up the dishes from supper before returning, but reckoned that would be too cruel.

Fallon had not moved an inch when she entered the parlor again, and the child retained her firm grip on his nose. He shot Jane a look of sheer panic. "Do thomthing! Thee won' leggo."

With great resolve, Jane maintained her composure and gently pried the little fingers away.

"Ga!" the babe protested as she was carried to her basket. "Ga ga. Goo!"

"I expect she has developed a fondness for you," Jane told Fallon when the infant was nestled under her soft blanket. Her eyes closed before Jane could murmur good night.

"She has a damnably odd way of showing it," Fallon said, rubbing his nose between his fingers. "What's more, she has a grip like a vise."

"You will recover, I expect." Jane smoothed her skirt with both hands. "And now, sir, we must put our heads together and determine how to proceed."

"It seems perfectly obvious to me. Unless you have something more for me to do here, I shall go after the perpetrators and haul them back to account for their actions."

"Very useful, to be sure."

He began to pace the room. "Well, *what* then? We can't let them get away with this."

"My lord, do remember that the infant was not cast away to die in the snow. She was left, very carefully, for us to find, which is quite a different matter."

"It's still a bloody crime! What the devil do they expect *us* to do with her?"

"Take better care of her than they were able, unless I am very much mistaken. There must have been a compelling reason for them to relinquish their beautiful, beloved daughter, and circumstances that made it impossible for them to do otherwise. We may never know the causes, sir. It is for us to deal with the situation as it stands."

He planted himself in front of her, hands clasped behind his back. "I'd wager they hadn't the money to raise the babe and passed her over to someone who does. Well, Miss Ryder, I do not consider that an acceptable solution to their problems. And if you are so convinced they wish to keep the child, all the more reason to find them immediately. Whatever is plaguing them, I'll put an end to it and send them off happily, infant in tow."

How like a man to assume there was a straightforward explanation and a simple solution for every difficulty, she thought. But life was rarely so uncomplicated as Lord Fallon imagined it was, or wished it to be.

"Were it only a matter of funds," she said patiently, "I expect they would have knocked on the door and begged you for a handout. In my heart, sir, I believe they had run out of choices before risking such a desperate undertaking as this." She gazed solemnly into his troubled eyes. "Perhaps they hoped for a miracle, sir, on this starry Christmas night."

After a moment he dropped onto a chair and beckoned her to sit across from him. "I don't believe in miracles," he said flatly. "I believe in hard work, fixed goals, and perseverance. But that is nothing to the point. If the infant's parents were looking for a Christmas angel, they appear to have found one. So tell me, Miss Ryder, what does heaven expect of you now? What are your instructions from the vast beyond, and how can I be of assistance?"

Her fingers curled around the arms of the chair. For all his bluster, Lord Fallon was dangerously close to sprouting wings. But he would be horrified to know what a soft-hearted, generous man he truly was, and she had no intention of being the one to tell him.

"I greatly wish," she said, choosing her words carefully, "that inspiration would strike at least one of us this very moment. But in my experience, heaven rarely draws maps. I fear we have been left to muddle through on our own, you and I. We do know one thing for certain. The child is now under our protection, and her welfare is our primary concern."

"Yes, yes," he agreed with a wave of his hand. "But what do we *do* with her?"

As if she knew! "To begin with, I expect you ought to head out at first light for the inn and recruit help from the

Wilkenses. Then we should return to London, I suppose. We cannot determine the best way to secure the infant's future without considerable thought, my lord. And I am sure you will attempt to trace her family before coming to any firm decision."

"What happens to her in London?" he demanded, invariably fixed on the most immediate problem to be solved.

"I shall take her with me to Lady Swann's house, if you have no objection."

"None whatever," he said, looking relieved. "Meantime, have *you* any objection if I go out now and follow the tracks leading from the stable while they are fresh? At the very least, I can get some idea which direction our miracle seekers have taken from here."

"If you must," she said with a sigh. "Mind you, the trail will be lost to you once they have turned onto a main road. But I imagine you'll not get any sleep, what with the babe requiring to be fed every few hours, so you may as well be gone."

Grumbling, he came to his feet and stomped to the door. "I'll check on the goat," he said. "And take a walk. If you need me, I'll be close enough to hear you call."

Wings and perhaps a halo, too, she thought as he vanished into the passageway.

Chapter 13

Pale dawn light crept over the snowfields, illuminating dark tree branches and barren shrubs, sending fingers of pink and gold into the clear azure sky. The landscape was unutterably still, as if all the world were holding its breath on this peaceful Christmas morning.

Fallon left the window and padded on stockinged feet to the couch where Jane lay asleep. One hand had escaped her blanket to curl around the edge of the willow basket on the floor close beside her.

The tiny protective gesture clutched at his heart.

After pulling on his boots, he buttoned his waistcoat and wrapped his neckcloth loosely around his throat. No telling what the Wilkenses would think when he appeared on their doorstep, unshaven and wearing patched trousers. Assuming, of course, that he could *find* their doorstep.

His tendency to get lost in the snow offended his vanity, as Jane Ryder would point out with one of her dimpled smiles—if she felt at liberty to tease him. Sometimes she forgot their difference in rank long enough to speak her mind, but not so often as he would have liked.

He stood for several moments gazing down at her face, soft with sleep, tendrils of her lovely hair drifting over her cheek. It was a face a man could look at, with pleasure, for a very long time.

"Miss Ryder," he whispered, gently touching her shoulder.

Her lashes flew open, and a brief frown of confusion wrinkled her brow. "The babe—?"

"All is well, my dear. I simply wished you to know that I am leaving now."

He realized that she was staring past him, with a startled expression, in the direction of the window. Spinning, he got the merest glimpse of a face staring back. Then it disappeared, and he saw a wiry figure bounding across the fields.

With an oath, Fallon blazed outside and took after the surprise caller on a run, following his tracks in the snow until he caught a flash of color through the trees. It was a young boy, he was certain, a fleet-footed and agile boy zigzagging around tree trunks and vaulting over fallen branches in a frenzied effort to escape.

Gradually Fallon's longer stride ate up the distance between them. "Stop!" he yelled. "I won't hurt you!"

With a new burst of speed, the boy leapt a gully and fled up a steep hill just beyond. His digging feet sent snow flying in the air, nearly blinding Fallon as he charged up the hill close behind.

When they reached the top, Fallon dived at the boy and seized him around the waist. Then, in a tangle of arms and legs, they rolled all the way down the other side of the hill, finally landing in a snowbank.

For a few moments they both lay still, panting, their breaths raspy in the winter quiet. Then the boy lashed out with fists and feet, spitting like a wildcat. Something, a heel perhaps, clipped Fallon's injured thigh.

"Hell confound it!" He rolled atop the boy and held him down. "Hit me again and you'll be sorry for it!"

Subsiding, the boy glared up at him. "Lemme go! You got no reason ter rag me. I ain't done nuthin' to you."

"That remains to be seen. What were you doing at the window?"

"I were passin' by an' saw smoke comin' from the chimneys. Reckoned I'd have a look-see. What of it?"

Fallon took a deep breath and counted to ten. "We'll continue this discussion inside, I think." Keeping hold of the boy's skinny arms, he stood and hauled him upright. "You can come with me peaceably, bantling, or be towed by the scruff of your neck. Which is it to be?"

"I'll go quiet," he said grudgingly. "You got m'word. And m'name ain't Bantling. It's Jed. But that's all I'm gonna say!"

"We'll see about that." He studied the boy's narrow freckled face, nodded, and released him, setting off toward the dower house without looking back. After a few moments, Jed caught up, slumping alongside with his hands stuffed in his pockets.

When they reached the parlor, Jane Ryder took one look at the wet, bedraggled boy and hustled him to the fire, cooing over him as if he were another helpless babe rescued from the snow instead of the scrappy spawn of the devil Fallon knew him to be.

But there was no mistaking the swift, urgent look he cast in the direction of the infant's basket. He knew bloody well who had left the child here and probably helped with the delivery, too. Now he'd come back, or someone had sent him back, to make sure the wicked Lord Fallon wasn't roasting the babe on a spit for his breakfast.

When Jane had settled the boy on a chair with a blanket wrapped around him, Fallon crossed to the hearth and draped his arm along the mantelpiece. "This is Master Jed," he said with a grim smile. "He happened to be passing by, so I invited him in for tea and a chat."

"I ain't done nothin'," Jed declared. "I ain't sayin' nuthin' neither, and you can't make me!"

"Don't be so sure, puppy. I expect Miss Ryder will not permit me to beat you, which would be the most expedient way to get at the truth. But I can certainly hand you over to the authorities for trespassing, not to mention attacking a lord of the realm."

"Wuz you attacked *me*!" Jed squawked. "Landed on me like a heap o' bricks, you did."

"Because you ran from the scene of the crime, which implies guilt in my book."

Jane cast him a dark look. "Oh, for heaven's sake, Fallon, do stop bullying the child. I'm sure he'll explain everything. Won't you, Jed?"

"Can't. Nuthin' to tell. I never done no crime, except mebbe stole some eggs an' the like."

Jane pulled up a tapestry footstool and sat beside the boy, turning the full force of her smile on him. "Do you live close by?" She took the nearest of his hands and rubbed it between hers. "How cold you are. Did you forget to wear your gloves?"

"Got no gloves. Don't need 'em."

"As it happens, I love to knit gloves. But I've run out of people to give them to. Will you mind if I knit you a pair one day? Any color you like, of course, but young men generally prefer brown."

"I likes brown," Jed conceded. "And I gots gloves, too, but they's yellow so I don't wear 'em. Only girls wears yellow."

"Exactly so. What strong hands you have, Jed. They will do credit to my knitting. But you must know that Lord Fallon has many questions to ask you, and just between us, I am sure you have all the answers he is looking for. He won't rest until he learns the truth, you know. Will it be easier if you tell me instead?"

Unsurprised, Fallon watched Jed crumble under her spell, no more able to resist that smile than any other red-blooded male on the planet. The boy's mutinous lips began to quiver, as if trying to hold back his secrets, and then he began to speak in a rush.

"I used ter work at the big 'ouse, 'til it were closed up. Now we lives mebbe two miles from here, me and Agathy. She were the old lord's 'ousekeeper. We oughtn't be there, she sez. We is t-tressin' or somethin'. You know, the word that 'un said." He jabbed a finger in Fallon's direction. "Agathy sez 'e'll toss us out on our ears when 'e knows about it." His shoulders slumped. "And now 'e does. But we didn't got nowheres else ter go."

Jane stroked the boy's cheek. "Well, you may be sure that Lord Fallon means to do nothing of the sort. Do you?"

After a moment Fallon realized that Jane was speaking to him. "Certainly not. I was notified some time ago that the former housekeeper had taken up residence in a cottage on the estate. I gave orders that she was not to be evicted."

"So you see," Jane said reassuringly, "everything will be perfectly all right."

"Don't see a bloody thing," Jed muttered sullenly. "I can't make no sense of anythin' 'e sez."

"Nor can I, a good deal of the time. Marquesses use a great many large words, I'm afraid, when small ones would serve as well. But I promise you, Agathy can live in that cottage for as long as she likes. In fact, I imagine Lord Fallon has also given orders to have it all fixed up so that you and Agathy will be warm and snug."

Jed brightened. "The roof leaks somethin' fierce, m'lady. And the winders are broke out. I nailed some wood over, but the wind still comes in."

"Ah. He'll want to have a look, then, to see what needs to be done. Will you take us there?"

"Dunno." He scuffed his tattered shoe against the flagstone hearth. "Gotta ask Agathy first."

Fallon's patience had run out. What was all this moonshine about fixing up cottages? He was just about to take the boy by the ears and shake the truth out of him when a loud squeal erupted from the infant.

He looked over to see two tiny hands waving for attention. Then he looked back at Jane, astonished when she failed to rush over to the basket. Her gaze remained fixed on Jed's twitching face. He was pretending not to notice the cries, but he had begun to squirm under his blanket.

"My lord," Jane said softly, "will you see what is disturbing the child?"

"Me?" Fallon's elbow dropped off the mantelpiece. "How the deuce would I know?"

"Oh, she will tell you, one way or another. Most likely she is feeling neglected. Why don't you bring her over so that Master Jed can make her acquaintance?"

Certainly. As if Master Jed never had the opportunity before now. Muttering under his breath, Fallon went to the basket, lifted the blanket away, and tried to remember what Jane had told him about holding an infant. Support the head. Don't squeeze too hard.

That was all perfectly simple when she'd put the babe into his arms last night. Now he had no idea where to take hold. He dropped to one knee, considering the logistics. Two pudgy arms and legs were churning like windmills, and she was screeching like a banshee.

He shot Jane a look of desperation, but she remained wholly preoccupied with the boy. Jed seemed to find it easier to give over when it was only the two of them. He was twattling a mile a minute, but too softly for Fallon to hear a word over the infant's cries.

"Shhh," he instructed, astonished when the shrieks immediately turned to gurgles. Wide blue eyes regarded him curiously, as if waiting for his next pronouncement. "Very good," he said. "May I pick you up?"

"Ga," she replied. "Goo ga ga."

Taking that for permission, he slipped his hands behind her back and gingerly lifted her to his chest, remembering to settle her head on his right biceps. For a moment she lay quietly in his arms, staring at his face, evaluating the situation.

Then a hand half the size of his thumb shot up and seized his nose.

"Wretched female," he murmured, unaccountably

pleased that she seemed to recognize him. More precisely, she recognized his nose, although why it held such fascination he could not begin to imagine. She clung to it relentlessly, though. And when he'd managed to gently pry her fingers away, she brought in her other hand for reinforcements.

"Thopp that," he ordered to no avail. She had two nose-seeking hands to the one hand he had free to deal with them, and after a brief skirmish, he conceded her the field.

He glanced over to see Jane Ryder grinning at him. Jed was doubled over, laughing.

What the hell? Laughter rumbled in his chest, which seemed to please the babe enormously. Her grip tightened, and she batted at his whiskered chin with her other hand. He could have sworn she was laughing, too.

"Thee likth my nothe," he said, returning to the fireplace. It occurred to him that the infant had effectively prevented him from taking over Jed's interrogation.

"And a splendid nose it is," Jane said kindly. "You must forgive us for being amused."

Fallon nodded, or tried to. For such a tiny mite, the babe had a formidable grip. Were females permitted to wrestle, he thought, this one would be champion material.

Jane smiled at him. "While you were otherwise occupied, sir, Jed has explained to my satisfaction why he cannot disclose the information we seek. He has given his promise, you see, and a gentleman must always honor his word. But he has agreed to take us to the cottage and vouch that we are good sorts."

"Said I'd vouch fer *you*," Jed objected. "Not 'im. 'E's a Fallon."

"Yes, indeed. I cannot blame you for being suspicious. But this new Lord Fallon is a good sort, too, when you get to know him. On that you must trust me, Jed, until the pair of you are better acquainted." She brushed her hand over the boy's wiry red hair. "Then you will decide for yourself, man to man, if he merits your regard or your contempt."

Fallon silently passed her the crown. Was a time he thought himself a master negotiator, but Jane Ryder beat him out on every count. He consoled himself with the thought that he was not the only male dancing to her tune. Jed's face held the rapt expression of a visionary gazing upon an angel.

Jane stood and held out her hands to the infant. Immediately the babe let go his nose and reached in her direction, which put him firmly in his place. He was good enough company, until someone better came along.

When the child was nestled happily in her arms, Jane turned her back to Jed and spoke softly, as if she were murmuring to the babe. "Apparently Mistress Agathy knows more about this business than the boy does, my lord. I'm sure you have already guessed that Jed played his part last night, and he was certainly dispatched here to spy on us this morning. But if we hope to learn anything more, we must apply to Agathy. Tactfully," she added with a pointed look. "I expect she will be even less forthcoming than Jed, unless handled with great care. Perhaps it will be best if you remain here with the child while I go with Jed to the cottage."

Offended, he shook his head. "Do you imagine I cannot deal with the likes of a *housekeeper*? What is more, I'll not have you tramping two miles through the snow. No, Miss Ryder. You may safely leave this business to me."

An hour later Fallon sat stone-faced on a teetery wooden chair, drinking the tea Agathy had insisted on brewing and pretending not to mind that the two adult females in the room had forgot his very existence.

Heads bent together over the infant's basket, Jane and the plump, bran-faced housekeeper sat just beyond earshot,

147

gabbing away as if they'd known each other for a life-time. Meantime, and solely because Jane had expected him to charge in like an aristocratic bull, Fallon remained where he was put, fully resolved to be as patient and diplomatic as . . . well, somebody famous for being patient and diplomatic.

He was not altogether sure how she had convinced him to bring her along. Indeed, it was more likely that she permitted him to accompany her. "You may lead the horse," she'd told him as if conferring a great honor, and before he knew it, that was precisely what he was doing. With Jed bouncing alongside and Jane atop Scorpio with the babe in her arms, they had crossed the snowy fields to Agathy's cottage without incident—if he discounted the time he stumbled up to his waist in a gully.

Agathy was, he thought, very much like the squat thatched cottage she shared with young Jed. Except for a pair of sharp brown eyes, her face and body were distinctly bovine. He had almost expected her to moo when she was rumbling about, brewing up the tea and watching him cautiously, as if he were a wolf that had wandered into her grazing pasture. She had the look of someone in service all her life, and the strength of one who had seen and endured the worst life could serve up.

At long last Agathy broke away from Jane and lowered herself onto a three-legged stool, turning her impassive gaze in his direction.

He shot a "Help me!" glance at Jane, who only shrugged before returning her attention to the child. Jed was sitting cross-legged by the fire, devouring a hunk of buttered bread.

Well, dammit, *somebody* had to get to the point. "Who does that child belong to?" he demanded.

Agathy never blinked. "She belongs to nobody, exceptin' those who will take 'er in."

"Well, then," he persisted, "who were the *nobodies*

148

left her in the snow last night? Her parents, obviously, but where have they gone?"

"You got it all wrong, m'lord. And I ain't free to set you clear." She emitted a heavy sigh. "Me and Jedediah done promised to keep a watch on the babe and bring 'er here if'n you turned 'er off. Mind you, I can't raise 'er meself, bein' old like I am. When I took in Jedediah, 'e weren't no more than a toddler, but back then there was work to be had. Now we got nothin'. If you mean to leave the babe with us, we'll go to Chelmsford when the winter's done and find a home what cares fer orphans."

"That will not be necessary," he said curtly. "The child belongs with her family. If they abandoned her for lack of housing or employment, I shall provide whatever they need to raise her properly. But you must tell me where to find them."

" 'Er got no mama or papa to be found, m'lord, and that's a fact. She be all alone in the world."

"I see." *Damn!* This was not, as he had hoped, a simple matter of tracking down the babe's parents, compelling them to take her back, and giving them the means to do so. He set his teacup on the floor and circled the small room twice, wondering how to proceed.

Agathy might as well have been chewing her cud from the placid expression on her doughy face. She had said all she was going to say, unless he could find some way to prod her. For that matter, where was Jane Ryder when he needed her? Why insist on coming here if she didn't mean to help? Hell, she could cozen the truth from this recalcitrant old woman without batting an eyelash.

But he had told her that he could handle the situation, and she was, quite perversely, leaving him to do it.

Hands clasped tightly behind his back, he stomped to the center of the room and planted himself in front of Agathy. "You don't trust me," he said bluntly. "I cannot blame you. No one who knew my father would place the slightest confidence in his heir. Nevertheless, I appeal to

149

your concern for the child, for she is the only one who matters now. Help me do what is best for her."

Silence.

Agathy's steady, penetrating gaze all but stripped him naked. Holding his ground, he drew in a long, prayerful breath. "Please, madam. I am asking for your help."

Finally she brushed her hands on her apron. "The Fallons is devils. They killed the land and drove the people what cared for it away. But yer wife is kindly, I reckon, and happen she can hold you steady."

"She will," he affirmed, not daring to look at Jane.

"Like I said, me 'n' Jed is bound to hold our tongues. But I'll go one step the wrong way, may the Lord forgive me, and give over this much of what I'm sworn not to tell. You needs to be askin' your questions of Richard Barrow, m'lord. He was the one what put the babe inter your protection."

At last! With effort, he steadied his voice. "Where can I find him?"

"Dunno that you can. 'E's a seaman. Went off in a rush to Portsmouth to catch 'is ship. If it's gone by now, so is 'e."

Fallon pulled out his watch. Only twelve hours since Barrow left the child and set out, and Portsmouth was eighty miles distant. No sailor could afford to hire fresh horses on the journey, so there was still a good chance of overtaking him. "What ship?" he demanded, already itching to be on the chase.

Agathy rubbed her chin. "Don't recollect 'e ever said."

"I knows!" Jed sprang to his feet. " 'E told me all what it's like, seein' the world. She's named the *Virga*. Ships is females," he added wisely. "That's cuz they'd go ever' which way without good men to 'andle 'em. Richard told me that women needs—"

"That will do, Jed," Jane interrupted before he could spell out what it was that women needed. "Agathy, will you hold the babe while I speak privately with his lordship?"

"I mean to catch that ship," Fallon said as he followed her outside. "Don't try to talk me out of it."

"As if I could. But before you leave, we must decide where Nan and I are to stay while you are gone."

"Who?"

"The infant," she said patiently. "Agathy told me her name."

"Oh." He tried it on his tongue. "Nan. Not much of a name, Nan."

She laughed. "That's very much what Lady Swann said to me when I introduced myself. 'Jane. Not much of a name, Jane.'"

"I'm exceptionally partial to Jane," he said reflectively. "May I have your permission to use it when we are private together?"

What an odd thing to ask under the circumstances. But then, there would be few if any occasions for him to do so, once this extraordinary adventure was concluded. "As you wish, sir."

"Thank you." His brow knitted in a frown. "You and Agathy have been thick as thieves all morning. Did she tell you anything else I ought to know?"

"Nothing of importance." She put a hand on his sleeve. "If you hope to catch up with Mr. Barrow, we must move quickly. Jed can lead you to the inn, because I'm sure you'll want to stop there for a change of clothes. Oh dear. I wonder if your valet ever arrived with the luggage."

"Never mind that. We will go to the inn, of course. You will be safe there until my return, with all those Wilkenses to look after you and the ba—Nan. Or do you wish me to arrange transportation to London?"

And here it was. Jane cleared her throat, steeling herself to deal with his objections. "If you don't mind, sir, I greatly prefer to stay at the dower house. Jed can bring supplies on his sled, as he does for Agathy, and I expect he'll agree to remain overnight."

"Out of the question! I will not leave you in that

ramshackle house with only a pair of children for company. What if there's another storm?"

"Then we'll bring the goat inside and cozy up by the fire. But if it makes you feel more at ease, my lord, send one of the Wilkens lads to stay with us. And have him bring my portmanteau, if you will. I'll be glad of something clean to wear."

He rubbed the back of his neck. "Why the dower house, Jane? It makes no sense."

"I am persuaded it does, my lord, for a great many small reasons. Shall I put them out for debate, or would you prefer to be on your way without a row?"

"I *prefer*," he said between his teeth, "for you to obey me. But I am also realistic. The dower house it is, and from there I'll go with Jed to the inn and dispatch food, portmanteau, and the brawniest of Rollin Wilkens's sons for protection. Have I forgot anything?"

"Don't forget to shave," she said, smiling. "Set foot on the docks with that sinister beard and a press gang will cart you off to His Majesty's Royal Navy."

"I won't even ask how you know so much about the docks, Jane Ryder. And before you offer more needless advice, I promise not to bully the truth from Richard Barrow when I catch up with him. I, too, have been a common sailor, and we speak the same language."

"You will be the soul of tact, I am sure. But come, sir. We have much to do before you gallop off to Portsmouth. If you will fetch Scorpio, I'll rally Jed and Nan."

As he headed to the tree where he'd secured the horse, Jane stole a long, loving look at his back. Such a *good* man.

She would try hard not to hope he failed to reach Portsmouth before Richard Barrow sailed away, carrying Nan's secrets with him to stay forever hidden, please God. No one could possibly want the child so much, or love her more, than she already did.

Dare she dream, this Christmas morning, that Nan had been delivered into her hands for a reason? Could this miracle hold true?

Chapter 14

Three days after departing for Portsmouth, Fallon arrived back at the Black Dove Inn.

He stopped only long enough for a bath and a change of clothes, relieved to learn that all was well with Jane and the child. The Wilkenses were clearly besotted with Nan. The boys had taken turns carting Mrs. Wilkens's fresh bread, steak-and-kidney pies, and rabbit stew to the house, while the girls had sewn new gowns and caps for the baby.

Rollin Wilkens drew him aside just before he climbed atop Scorpio for the last stage of his journey. If no one else wanted the precious lamb, he said earnestly, the Wilkens family would be happy to take her in.

Although Fallon had ridden neck-or-nothing to Portsmouth and almost as swiftly on the return, pausing only to change horses and, once, to grab a few hours of sleep, he took the last few miles at a walk.

He had always considered himself a man of decisive action, but it seemed forever that his mind had been turning cartwheels, examining the situation from every possible angle. And when he approached the dower house, he was no closer to finding an answer than when he first understood the nature of the problem.

What was he to tell Jane? *How* was he to tell her?

Above all, what was he to *do*?

Jed was in the stable playing with the goat when Fallon led Scorpio inside. He rushed over to take the reins, his freckled face blazing with excitement. "Miz

Jane sez I c'n keep the goat, if'n you sez yes. I named 'er Peg. I do all the milkin' now, 'n' feed 'er, and clean the stall. C'n I 'ave 'er, yer lordship? Pleeeeze?"

Good Lord, what next? With a shrug, Fallon began to unsaddle the horse. "I see no reason why not, once Peg is free of her current duties."

"Miz Jane sez there's no place in Lunnon fer a goat," Jed informed him. "An' if Peg lives with me 'n' Agathy, I won't be needin' to fetch milk from Rumford."

"We'll see, young man." Fallon tossed the saddle over the stall gate. "How are things at the house? Have there been any difficulties?"

"No sir. 'Ceptin' Miz Jane makes me . . . well, she sed Claude Wilkens wuz too clumsy and she 'ad to sleep sumtimes, so she taught me ter . . ." He shuddered.

"I believe I get the picture, Jed. You have all my sympathy."

"Ain't so bad when I 'old m'nose, but I needs both 'ands to tie the knots. An' sumtimes Nan poops agin afore I's even done. Miz Jane sez it's never too soon fer a man to learn, sir, but I been thinkin' it's the females what's supposed to do them jobs."

"An opinion I heartily share. But here's another lesson for you, Jed. Females have a way of getting a man to do whatever they want him to do. Things no man ever thought about doing, things he was sure he'd *never* do—until he finds himself doing them. You may as well get used to it."

"Oh, I 'spect t'go to sea one day, m'lord. No females there."

"Not a one," Fallon agreed. Jed would discover soon enough that there was another side to that coin. A lonely side. "Give Scorpio a good rubdown, will you?"

"Yessir." Jed shifted from one foot to the other. "Did y'find 'im, m'lord?"

"I did."

"Then y'know 'bout Nan. An' the rest."

"Yes. I believe, too, that I've put his mind at ease concerning the child, so it's as well that Agathy gave me his name and direction." He smiled. "I assured Mr. Barrow that you kept your word to him, Jed. He said that he expected nothing less of you."

"I alius keep m'word. That's what tells the gentl'men from the scoundrels, Agathy sez."

Fallon put his hands on the boy's narrow shoulders. "I want you to go on keeping it, Jed."

He nodded wisely. "I unnerstands, m'lord. You kin trus' me."

"So I do. And I wish to be private with Miss Jane for the next hour or two, so if any Wilkenses show up—"

"I'll 'ead 'em off, sir."

As he left the stable, Fallon realized that Richard Barrow and Master Jed, commoners both, were two of the most honorable gentlemen he had ever met.

When he let himself into the house, a cold sweat broke out on his forehead at the thought of what awaited him. He leaned against the closed door to gather his wits.

They refused to be gathered.

Finally deciding that he could stand there well into the next millennium without any better idea how to proceed, he ordered his feet to take him to the parlor.

They had carried him only a short way down the hall when he heard the sound of giggling and a soprano voice singing decidedly off-key. He paused at the open parlor door and looked inside.

Jane, her long hair tied back with a green ribbon to match her dress, was holding Nan under her little arms and swooping her up and down as she twirled around the room. "Nan's a bird," she sang, dipping and swaying, the babe giggling deliriously. "Nan's a bird. Nan can fly, she can, she can. Nan's a flying bird."

Her whirling dance carried her toward the door, still singing until she glanced up and met his eyes. She stumbled to a halt then, and drew Nan into a protective embrace. The babe squealed in protest. "Sh-she likes the flying game," Jane said as Nan's squeal turned into a wail.

"I can see that." Heart pounding, he stepped into the room and closed the door behind him. "And so do you."

At the sound of his voice, Nan stopped crying and turned in his direction, flailing her arms. "Ga! Ga ga ga ga!"

Rather sure that *ga* was her private word for *nose*, Fallon kept his own well out of reach as he came closer, offering her a finger to tug on instead. She immediately brought it to her mouth and began sucking.

This close to Jane, her wide hazel eyes regarding him solemnly, or perhaps fearfully, he felt a swarm of unfamiliar emotions rush over him. His vision blurred and his tongue tied itself into a knot. What to say? *Oh God, Jane, what am I to do?*

Gently she pried his finger from Nan's mouth. "You found Richard Barrow, my lord?"

He nodded.

"Well, then, I expect you've a great deal to tell me. And you must be very tired. Claude Wilkens once traveled to Portsmouth, and he assured me you could not possibly return before tomorrow night. But then, he does not know you well." She smiled. "I had him fetch another bottle of brandy from Wolvercote, by the way. It's over there on the sideboard. Or would you rather I brewed some coffee?"

He nodded. He couldn't seem to force himself to do any more than that. Bless Jane for understanding, for clearly she did.

With dazzling efficiency, she soon had Nan settled peacefully in her basket and him out of his greatcoat and seated by the fire with his feet propped on a footstool. She placed the open bottle of brandy and a glass on a small table by his side.

He could not begin to imagine what she was thinking. Her expression remained calm, her manner unruffled, and gradually he let himself relax because she wanted

157

him to. She even said so, very softly, as she put a cushion behind his head.

"Do relax, my lord, while I prepare the coffee. Would you like something to eat?"

He shook his head.

"Just as well," she said, patting his sleeve. "This morning I had another go at baking gingerbread men, but even Jed could not choke them down. I mean to save them, though. More roof tiles for Wolvercote."

When she was gone, he poured a glass of brandy with shaking hands and sipped it slowly, heat burning down his throat as he stared into the fire.

"Ga," Nan proclaimed from her basket.

Ga indeed. It won't be so easy, he thought, when you have heard the truth. Will you speak to me then, Nan? Will you grab my nose and suck my finger when you know who I am? Or will I ever tell you?

In the kitchen, Jane placed sugar and a dish of fresh cream on the tray beside the pot of coffee, belatedly remembered the napkins, and closed her eyes for a moment to compose herself.

Lord Fallon had something unpleasant to tell her, she knew. No, not *unpleasant*. Something horrible, something that had shuttered his eyes and made him wary of looking at her. Something that wrenched at his heart.

She didn't want to hear it. For three days and nights she had lived in a dream world of her own, imagining and hoping and praying. But she had realized, the moment she saw his face, that what she longed for could never be.

There was no use delaying the inevitable, though, and bad news never got better for putting it off. Murmuring a prayer for strength, she picked up the tray and returned to the parlor.

Fallon gave her a faint smile as she handed him a cup of coffee. "Will you sit close by, Jane? This is going to be a long story, I'm afraid, as confusing to hear as it is difficult to tell. I cannot think where to begin."

"With Richard Barrow, if you will." She dropped a thick cushion near the hearth and sat cross-legged, hands clenched in her lap. "What sort of man is he?"

"As Jed would say, a good 'un. Not much older than twenty, I would guess, average height, plain in appearance. When I arrived, the *Virga* was near to getting under way, but the captain gave me leave to take Barrow from his duties for a short while. We found a quiet place at the end of the wharf and spoke for perhaps twenty minutes." Fallon laced brandy into his coffee. "Under the circumstances, he could give me only an abbreviated version of events, and I neglected to ask many questions that came to mind after his departure. Unfortunately, the *Virga* is bound for New South Wales, so it will be a long time before I get the answers."

Jane could not wait for the one answer she had to have immediately. "Did he tell you about Nan's parents? Are they alive?"

"Her mother is dead," he replied in a suffocated tone. "Barrow never learned the father's identity. She is, for all purposes, an orphan."

Burningly aware of a profound and shameful sense of relief, she looked over at the basket where Nan lay sleeping. Only the top of her knitted cap was visible, but Jane imagined she could see the sweet little face and mischievous eyes. "Do continue, my lord. I'll not interrupt you again."

"Do so if you wish, but meanwhile I'll give you the story as Barrow gave it me. He had six weeks of leave and was on his way to Sheffield when he came upon a pony cart that had lost a wheel. The driver was a young woman, painfully thin and obviously quite ill. She had with her a shabby traveling bag, a goat, and an infant. Barrow fixed the wheel and insisted on driving her to the nearest town with a physician in residence.

"With that act of kindness, his odyssey began. The lad never did get home to see his family." Fallon took a drink of coffee. "At length, they found a doctor, although he could do little for the young woman but make her comfortable. It had been a difficult childbirth, he guessed, from which she never fully recovered. With care, she would surely have done so, but she had evidently been traveling for a long time. Exhaustion, winter cold, and insufficient food had weakened her past all hope. Three days later, she was dead."

"Dear Lord," Jane murmured. "Where was her home? Where were her family?"

"Although fevered and sometimes delirious, she told Barrow something of what had occurred. Her name was Margaret, by the way. I'm afraid parts of her story will be familiar to you, for she, too, was the daughter of a careless aristocrat and one of his servants. But unlike your father, he cast off his mistress and daughter without a penny. Barrow never learned what happened in the years after that, except that Margaret took a position as a kitchen maid in Coventry after her mother died."

Jane could well imagine what she had endured all those missing years. But unlike Margaret, she had been provided an education and a secure childhood. There were troubles enough later on, but in comparison, her own life had been a virtual picnic.

Fallon took up the story again. "An infantry regiment was training recruits near to Coventry, and Margaret fell in love with one of the young soldiers. She was very specific about that, Barrow said. She loved him, and he'd promised to marry her as soon as his father and the commanding officer gave permission. But when she told him they were to have a child, he said marriage was out of the question. Soon after, he was dispatched to the Peninsula and never contacted her again. Since Margaret refused to give his name, I doubt Nan will ever know her father's identity."

"She's well rid of him!" Jane declared. "What use is a father who rejects his own child before she's even born?"

"I rather hope he'll be used as cannon fodder," Fallon said. "Maybe the French will do England a service for once and purge this wastrel from the ranks. As for Margaret, she went off to beg help from her mother's family. They had turned off their daughter years before, but agreed to let Margaret stay with them until the babe was delivered. Three months after, they sent her off with eight shillings, a cart, a pony, and the goat. In return for this largesse, she was made to swear that she would never return."

Despite the fire at her back, Jane felt cold to the bone. She wrapped her arms around her waist. How could people be so cruel to one another? "I should like to find those heartless beasts," she said, "and tear them limb from limb."

"As would I, more than you can know. In any event, Margaret set off on a desperate journey south, to plead with her father for assistance. By then she must have known she was dying, else she'd not have grasped for a straw in the wind. Barrow said that she was obsessed with finding him and kept demanding that she be allowed to climb aboard her cart and continue the search. He was Nan's only hope, she insisted. She meant to approach him Christmas morning, certain he would not turn Nan away on that holiest of days."

"No more could we," she said, arrested at the thought. "Is that why—"

"In part," Fallon said. "It was Margaret's faith in a Christmas miracle that gave Barrow the idea, to be sure. For the rest, we happened to be there, and he had run out of options by then. He gave Margaret his word, you see, that he would find a home for Nan. He stayed with her the last night of her life, promising again and again, not certain she could even hear him. But at the end, while he was sitting beside her with Nan in his arms, she opened her eyes and reached for her child. She appeared to be lucid, Barrow said. She stroked the babe's cheek, and thanked Barrow for his kindness, and when he made his promise yet again, she smiled. A few minutes later, she was gone."

Jane pressed her wrist to her mouth to keep from sobbing aloud. Tears poured down her cheeks.

Save for the crackling fire, the room went silent for a long time. Finally Jane regained control of herself, using her skirt to wipe her face. Unable to look at Fallon quite yet, she turned on her cushion and placed another log on the fire.

When she turned back, he was gazing directly at her, his face somber, his eyes shimmering. Were those tears, she wondered? He was deeply affected, she was certain, but only a man with a heart of stone could fail to be.

"The rest is not so painful to hear," he assured her, rubbing the back of his neck. "But it was painful enough for Mr. Barrow, who spent much of what he'd saved from his wages to pay the physician and see Margaret buried in the parish churchyard. He never mentioned the money, of course, until I asked if there were debts to be settled. He said not, but it was clear that by the end of his journey, he was at very low tide indeed.

"He went first in search of Margaret's father, as he'd sworn to do. But the man was dead, devil take him, so Barrow cast about for a decent family willing to take Nan in and love her. He was a stranger in a strange land, though, with little idea where to begin. Mind you, he skimmed briefly over this part of the story, but I knew from his voice and the look in his eyes that he had met a good deal of rejection along the way."

"No room at the inn," Jane murmured.

"In a way, yes. Although if he'd stumbled across the Black Dove Inn, the Wilkenses would have welcomed him immediately. They have offered to adopt Nan into the family, you know. Indeed, they are eager to do so. But it was Jed he chanced to meet, in Rumford, where the boy goes twice a week to buy food and supplies. Jed took Barrow and Nan home to Agathy, who agreed to care for the child while he continued his search. Because Agathy's cottage is small, Barrow slept here in the dower house when he wasn't on the road. He sold the cart and pony to hire a job horse, so that he could make faster time between villages."

"What a remarkable man," Jane said. "I wish I could have met him."

"I am privileged to have had that opportunity," Fallon agreed. "He will write me if he thinks of anything else I should know and has promised to contact me the next time his ship makes port in England. You may be sure I'll find a way to repay him—without insulting his pride, of course—for all he has done for Margaret and Nan." He reached for the coffeepot.

"The coffee must have gone cold by now, sir. Shall I brew some fresh?"

He shook his head. "Everything tastes like mud at this point, even the brandy. Besides, I'm nearly done with Barrow's story. He fled the dower house when my agents came poking around the estate. By then he had despaired of finding Nan a home in a nearby town, and his ship was due to sail within a few days, so he went off to London and investigated the foundling homes there. I won't tell you what he had to say of them, but I am resolved to use what little influence a Fallon may have in the Lords, along with my own financial resources, to improve conditions in those appalling warehouses."

Jane nodded, aware he would not wish to be praised for what any decent man with the means to help would do. At the same time, a glimmer of hope rose again in her heart. Nan remained, as Agathy had said, all alone in this world. Well, not altogether, for Fallon would never abandon her. But what would a bachelor aristocrat do with an infant? And when he took an aristocratic wife, would she welcome an orphan into her aristocratic home? Not likely! The glimmer of hope flamed brighter.

"By now," Fallon said, "you have guessed the rest. Barrow, on his way back from London, sheltered at a post house during the storm that brought us to the dower house. When it abated, he was on his way to Agathy's cottage when he chanced to see me riding around. Lost,"

163

he added with a rueful grin. "You recall that I went exploring on Christmas Eve. Barrow followed me to the dower house, saw you through the window, and hit upon his plan to leave Nan by the stable for us to find."

"Did he know who you were? I mean, who you *are*?"

There was a long silence. Fallon's face had gone pale, and his hand trembled as he set the cup in its saucer. "Not for certain, Jane, but he had guessed. He rallied Jed to help, brought Nan and the goat to the stable, and when everything was arranged, he rang the bell to get our attention. The bell had used to be around the goat's neck, he told me. He forgot to leave it when he went off to hide with Jed and wait for us to come out. It was you turned the trick, of course. When he saw how you took Nan up in your arms, he was convinced she had found a home. Then, with little time to spare, he mounted his horse and left to catch his ship. Jed had promised to keep an eye on us and rescue Nan if she looked in need of rescuing."

He leaned his head back, eyes closed. "And that is what I learned from Mr. Barrow," he said wearily. "You know what happened after that."

But she hadn't heard the whole of it, Jane knew in her heart. After the urgent ride to Portsmouth, and the racking story he had related to her, Fallon was burned down to coals. But he felt a pain far deeper than he had confessed. It had been in his eyes when first she saw him standing at the parlor door, and grew immeasurably more profound as he spoke.

She studied his face, the lines of fatigue at his temples and the corners of his mouth, the long thick eyelashes, the muscle ticking at his jaw. He was so much alone, she thought, even more alone than she. He had no one at all to confide in. To be sure, he was not a man to acknowledge his feelings to himself, let alone share them with anyone else. If he had wanted her to know, he would have told her.

Or perhaps he wanted to and didn't know how. She

risked nothing to ask, save a rebuff, and heaven knew she'd survived her share of those over the years.

"What more, my lord?" she began hesitantly. "Will you tell me?"

She heard the breath rasp in his throat and his eyes opened, glowing like molten amber in the firelight. "You *are* a witch," he said softly. "I have always known it. And I was a fool to think I could hide the truth from you. I'm not altogether sure why I tried, except that the words are so vastly hard to say. But I don't mind if you know, Jane. I won't even ask you not to tell Lady Swann, for I am sure you will understand why this must not become common gossip. For Nan's sake, mind you, not my own."

He ran his fingers through his hair. "Perhaps you can help me decide if she ought to be told, when she is old enough to understand. Or tell me what to do beginning to end, Jane, for God knows I haven't the slightest notion where to go from here."

Unable to think of anything to say, she knelt forward and placed a hand on his thigh. In response he brushed his fingers against her cheek.

"Nan is not altogether without blood family," he said. "When Margaret went in search of her father, she was looking for *my* father. She was my sister, Jane. My half sister, not to put too fine a point on it, and born after I had gone sailing off on the *Petrel*. Hell confound it, if only I had *known* about her."

Pulse hammering in her veins, she forced herself to remain calm. All this time, as he was telling her what she thought was the heartbreaking story of a stranger, he had been speaking of his own sister. Dear God. She could scarcely breathe for wanting to take him in her arms.

"You must not punish yourself," she said gently. "You could not have known. Who was there to tell you?"

"Indeed. I have been trying to convince myself for the past twenty or so hours that I am not to blame. But what has logic to say about what happened to her? I was here

165

in England when Margaret set off in her pony cart with Nan. While I was choosing a town house and being measured by Weston for coats and waistcoats, she was dying."

Nothing she could say would make a difference, Jane knew. Still stroking her hair, he gazed over her shoulder into the fire.

"In the spring," he said finally. "I'll go to where she is buried and place a marker on her grave. She must not be forgot, Jane." Conceiving of something to do, some action to take, seemed to revive him. He let go her hair and stood, clearly needing to be in motion. "I shall care for Nan, of course. She'll come back with me to London. The servants can fix up a nursery, and my solicitor will employ a suitable nanny, or whatever it is she requires." When his pacing carried him past the basket, he paused to gaze down at the sleeping child. "Damn if I know what that is."

Heart galloping in her chest, Jane rose and clutched at her skirts with both hands. "The very *last* thing she needs, my lord, is to be raised by servants and hired nurses."

He looked over at her with a frown. "You think she will do better if I find a family to take her in? But how could I be sure of them? I cannot pluck a suitable family out of a hat. Even the Wilkenses, who would certainly treat her well, are barely literate. She ought to be educated, don't you think?"

"Certainly. But have you considered what will happen a few weeks or months from now, when you go in search of a wife? I know you mean to do so. Will your bride accept Nan into the family and raise her as an equal with your children?"

He stalked to the fireplace and jabbed at the logs with a poker. "I had not considered. But why would she mind? Marriages among my class are based solely on alliances of titles, connections, fortunes—even political aspirations. We will be entering a business arrangement, after all."

"A marriage of convenience."

"Precisely. Since I already have the title and the fortune, I seek a wife with the proper connections. Her reputation and the influence of her family will go a long way to restoring the Fallon name, which has been my goal from the beginning." He grimaced. "It sounds damnably bloodless when spoken aloud, does it not?"

"It is a laudable goal, sir, and I am persuaded you ought not turn back when you are so near to achieving it. But I see no place for Nan in that picture. Indeed, she would be a constant reminder of your family's disgraceful history, and I would not be in the least surprised if people concluded that she was your own bastard daughter. How did you mean to explain her to your bride, and to everyone else?"

"Obviously I had not thought that far ahead. But dammit, Jane, she is my niece. I cannot cut her loose on my own account. And who is to say that a woman courageous enough to marry a Fallon will not also accept the child?"

"And love her in the bargain?" Jane shook her head. "I am no gamester, my lord, but the odds against that seem overwhelming to me."

The poker dropped from his hand, clattering against the hearth. Head bowed, he stood gazing down at it. "What am I to do then?" he murmured. "I once asked you, Jane, to be my conscience in reserve when my own failed me. Well, it is certainly failing me now."

"I believe, sir, that you cannot come to any reasonable conclusion while you are driven by guilt. Long ago, you set yourself to dredge your family back into respectability. I am not convinced you give tuppence for what Society thinks of you, but I respect you for choosing a worthwhile goal and pursuing it with diligence."

"Do you? Then why have I the feeling you are ripping me to pieces with every word you say? Make no mistake, I accept not a hair of responsibility for the crimes of my family. But I did inherit responsibility for the future, and that is a charge I have always accepted. Do you expect me to let it go for the sake of a child?"

"Do *you*?"

"Dammit, Jane, you are supposed to be advising me."

"Then let us come to the point, sir. Why do you wish to take Nan into your household and acknowledge your relationship, even though that would put the both of you in an impossible situation?"

He stood rigid and silent.

"You will not betray your sister, my lord, by choosing Nan's happiness above all things. And that is what Margaret would want you to do." She came to his side. "It is, in the end, the only honorable course to take."

"I would do so in a heartbeat," he said tightly, "were there such a course mapped out for me. But damned if I see one, Jane."

She put her hand on his arm. "You can give her to me."

For a long time, he didn't move. She imagined he had ceased to breathe, so very still he was. Then, turning slowly, he gazed steadily into her eyes. *Oh, please,* she begged him silently. *Please.*

"You love her," he said simply.

"Oh, yes." All the words she had stored up while he was gone came rushing out. "I love her with all my heart. I shall be a good mother to her, I promise. And I've thought it all out, sir. I'll find a little house somewhere, in a small town perhaps, where she'll have lots of playmates. There are many widows from the war who are raising children on their own. No one will question that Nan's father went to the Peninsula and never came back. It's partly true, after all. And I know you will see to it there is money for her schooling, and a dowry. And—"

He placed his forefinger gently over her lips. "You needn't try to convince me, Jane. You love her, and that's enough."

Tears welled in her eyes. "I may have her, then?"

"To be sure." He brushed a tear from her cheek. "I only wish Margaret could have known that her child found such a one as you to care for her."

"I believe she does know, my lord. I shall never credit this all came about by sheerest accident. She delivered Nan into my hands, as well as yours, on Christmas night."

"Perhaps you are right, although I was never one to put stock in miracles." He cleared his throat, plainly uncomfortable with the subject. "I think we must be practical now and decide how to proceed from here. Or"—he raised a brow—"have you already made up your mind?"

She could not help a watery chuckle. He knew her so very well. "As a matter of fact, sir, I do have a few suggestions. If you will arrange transportation, I'll take Nan with me to London. We can stay with Lady Swann until a suitable house is found, and there is no reason to make a hurried decision. It will be better to move in the spring, I expect."

"Why not let me build you a house here at Wolvercote? That way I can—"

"No, my lord." She drew herself up. "That would be most unwise. When Nan is older, you and I will discuss what she should be told of her real mother, and of her uncle. On that matter, I have no idea what will be best. But I do know how it felt to grow up on the fringes of a grand estate, provided for by his lordship and a pariah to his wife, wondering why it was they could not love me. I'll not have Nan think, as I did, that there is something wrong with her, something in her nature that makes her unworthy of affection."

"I see. Well, I do *not* see, but I trust your judgment." His eyes searched her face. "Do you mean to cut me off from her altogether, Jane?"

"I believe," she said, choosing her words with care, "that we must get our lives in order, separately, before making that decision. You will soon be preoccupied with rebuilding Wolvercote, sir, and selecting a wife, and caring for your own children. I shall write to you, if you wish, and tell you how Nan is getting on. Otherwise, it is best we put distance between us for now. And to that end, I suggest you turn over the matter of financial arrangements to your solicitors."

"You'd rather deal with a bloody *lawyer* than with me? Good God, what's the point of that? You know I'll give you whatever you ask."

"And a great deal more, I expect." She regarded him earnestly. "You must let go, Lord Fallon, and permit others to act in your stead. Of all things, nothing could be more difficult for you. I do understand. And I cannot think how to convince you that what I ask will be best for all of us."

Nor can I tell you, she thought as he looked at her with troubled eyes, *how much it hurts me to be with you when I cannot have you. For Nan's sake, you must leave us alone or I shall be torn to pieces from wanting you.*

He slipped his warm fingers around her hand and led her across the room. Together they gazed down at the infant, sleeping the sleep of the rapturously innocent.

"It will be as you wish, Jane," he said quietly. "I'll not interfere. But, dear Lord, how I shall miss her."

Chapter 15

When Larch delivered the afternoon post to his study, Fallon was surprised to find a letter from Richard Wellesley.

He had returned early to London, Wellesley explained, for strategy meetings regarding a bill he meant to propose. A few of his political cronies had also arrived, some with families in tow, and none were eager to work this last day of the Christmas season. Instead, they had decided to stage an impromptu Twelfth Night celebration and requested Lord Fallon's presence should he chance to be free this evening.

In his sly way, Wellesley had included a partial list of the guests, and Fallon immediately recognized two names. Those same two ladies were prominently featured on his own list of potential brides. He chuckled. Wellesley, determined to recruit him on the side of the angels, would be delighted to see him marry into a loyal Tory family—even to the point of playing matchmaker.

Fallon glanced at the mantelpiece clock, which showed a little past two. There was no reason *not* to join Wellesley and his friends, beyond the familiar sense of dread that squeezed at his insides. There would be many such evenings in the future, he knew, evenings spent making small talk with strangers, vetting the season's crop of eligible females, and trying to ignore the sidelong looks cast in his direction.

There goes the Fallon heir. Hide your daughters.

Best to begin slowly, he supposed, at tonight's small

gathering, with Wellesley to guide him. And it wasn't as if he'd anything better to do. Since returning to London, he had spoken to no one other than his starchy servants and his solicitors. He left the house only to exercise Scorpio in Hyde Park and shake off his own black moods in the crisp winter air. One was on him now, as he reached for paper and pen to send Wellesley a note of acceptance.

"M'lord?" Larch appeared at the door, his gaunt face a portrait of indignation. "An excessively odd person insists . . . er, has requested to speak with you."

Fallon set down his pen with an exasperated groan. "And has he a name, Larch?"

"I expect that *she* does, m'lord. But when I inquired as to what it might be, she directed that a pair of footmen be dispatched to carry her up the stairs. She is waiting on the pavement, you see."

Lady Swann. It could be no one else. His stomach began to churn. Dear God, something terrible must have happened to Jane or the infant. Only a true catastrophe would bring the old lady here in person.

He drew a steadying breath. "See that she is made comfortable in the drawing room, Larch, and provide her with a cup of tea. I'll join her in a few minutes."

Images of disaster wheeled in his head as he waited long enough for Lady Swann to be settled. She was a proud woman, and he reckoned she would not wish him present while the servants carted her into the house. Even so, the short time he paced the study felt like centuries as he imagined every possible horror that could befall a young woman or a fragile babe. Unable to wait a moment longer, he practically ran down the passageway, arriving just as Larch was making a hasty exit from the drawing room, followed by a maid carrying a tray.

"Never mind the sherry," Lady Swann called out. "I'd rather brandy. *Good* brandy."

The butler's thin brows were set in a disapproving frown. "She has refused the tea, m'lord."

172

"Then bring her whatever she wants, Larch." *Numb-skull,* he added under his breath, bracing himself to enter the room. When he did, closing the door behind him, he saw Lady Swann ensconced in her Bath chair, which had been pulled close to the fireplace.

"About time you got here," she complained, raising her lorgnette. "And wherever did you unearth that nincompoop of a butler?"

She was smiling. A surge of intense relief made jelly of his legs. There could be no disaster, at least not of the kind he had feared. Lady Swann herself was a disaster on wheels.

"Come, come, rascal. If you don't mean to do the pretty, ask me straight out why I have gone to considerable trouble for a private coze with you."

At the blunt reminder that he'd forgot his manners, he made a perfunctory bow. "Dare I hope, Lady Swann, it is to tell me you've changed your mind about publishing your scurrilous book?"

"No. And if I had, I shouldn't bother to notify *you*." Her expression hardened. "Much the way you have not bothered these last eight days and nights to inquire after Miss Ryder and the child."

"My solicitors are in daily contact with Miss Ryder," he said stiffly. "Their reports have given me no reason for concern."

"And when those same lackeys have established Jane and Nan in some distant province where they cannot prove an embarrassment, you need not give them another thought."

"Miss Ryder is free to live wherever she chooses," he corrected. "And wherever that is, she will want for nothing. I have made certain of it. What is more, it is by her own wish that our business is conducted through my solicitor. I was more than willing to handle it personally."

"Don't insult me, boy. I understand the situation very well. You mean to buy them the best of everything, and by doing so, buy off your own conscience. An excellent bargain," she said with awful sarcasm. "For *you*."

Miserable old woman, he thought savagely. What did she know of it? And if his conscience chanced to gnaw at him on occasion, it was none of her bloody business. Besides, Jane insisted they were both doing the only thing that could be done. It was best for everyone, she had said. It was what she wanted.

His tumultuous thoughts were interrupted by Larch's arrival with a decanter of brandy.

"Fallon will do the pouring," Lady Swann instructed the butler sharply. "Leave us."

He had never seen Larch move so quickly, Fallon thought as the butler scurried out the door. Crossing to the sideboard, he filled two snifters with brandy and gave one to Lady Swann. "I am persuaded you will eventually come to the point, madam. However, know in advance that Miss Ryder and I have satisfactorily agreed to terms, and that I mean to disclose none of the details. If you require information or explanations, you must apply to her."

"Turn my chair," she said. "I wish to face the hearth. And you may park yourself by the mantelpiece where I can see you."

Which effectively pinned him in, he realized when he'd done her bidding. While she had been facing the other direction, he was free to prowl the room. But trapped between her piercing gaze and the fire, he could only stand in place, which always made him wildly uncomfortable.

Clever woman. He admired her tactics. He wished there were no laws against tossing crippled old ladies off balconies.

She took a long drink of brandy, regarding him with a steady, unnerving gaze that made him wonder if she could see through his clothing. Through his skin, for that matter. He felt her nosing at his very bones.

"Excellent brandy," she pronounced. "But the Fallons always did have a partiality for drink. Do you tipple to excess, boy?"

"Now and again," he replied equably. What the devil had his drinking habits to do with her? "In general, I prefer to retain control of my wits."

"I daresay what few you possess require constant supervision," she said with an arched brow. "But I am pleased to hear you have not inherited that particular Fallon vice. Now pay attention, for I am about to tell you something of importance, even though I must break a confidence to speak of it."

"Indeed?" He propped an elbow on the mantel. "But how is that of consequence, Lady Swann? You are scarcely known for keeping secrets."

She barked a laugh. "Touché, rascal. There may be hope for you yet. But here is my news. Monday next, Jane Ryder means to depart London and take up residence at a small house I own in Bibury."

He nearly dropped his glass. "I d-don't understand. We agreed she would move in the spring, to the house I intend to buy for her. And by all accounts, she has not yet made up her mind where she wishes to live."

"True. But while she considers, she wishes to put distance between you and the child. She is afraid, you see, that you will reconsider your decision to leave Nan in her care."

"But that is absurd. I have given my promise. And were I scoundrel enough to break it, I could easily chase her down." He felt a heavy lump clogging his throat. "She has no reason to hide from me."

"So I have told her. 'Tis all nonsense, of course. The last thing you wish is a Fallon by-blow on your doorstep."

"That's not the point!" He realized he was shouting. "Why did you come here to tell me this?" he asked more softly. "Naturally I regret that Miss Ryder is disturbed for no reason, but if she prefers to decamp to Bibury, so

175

be it. My solicitors can easily deal with her there. I trust you will provide me her direction."

"Why, what a pompous twit you have become, Fallon. And in so brief a time." Lady Swann shook her head. "When first we met, I imagined you had some spine in your back. I'd never have taken such trouble putting the two of you together had I known you to be such a thatch-gallows. But it becomes painfully clear that Jane Ryder is wasted on you, sir. For all my scheming, she will do better on her own."

Fallon swiped his fingers through his hair, feeling just about as stupid as she thought him to be. "What the devil are you talking about? You cannot have planned that we would be stranded together in a snowstorm, or that Richard Barrow would deposit an infant in our laps." Or could she? He was beginning to wonder.

"Ah, 'twas pure serendipity, the storm and the babe," she said reflectively. "Or perhaps Heaven itself chose to conspire with me. I wonder the good Lord failed to realize you would not recognize a miracle when it dropped into your hands. He ought to have sent an archangel along to thwap you upside the head."

He must have done, Fallon thought. Why else would his mind be spinning as if a mule had kicked him?

"I see that I must lead you through this maze one step at a time," she said with a quelling look. "I had been certain one of you would come to your senses, with no help from me, before it was too late. But Jane has both heels dug in, and is fearful besides. I cannot appeal to her. She is too busy trying to protect the child—and you."

"Protect *me*? Whatever from?"

"Scandal, on the surface of it. But at bottom, she is determined to indulge your own folly. She wants you to have everything you think you want—marriage to a proper wife in a proper house while you lead a proper life. Pah. As if you were the least bit capable of dancing to Society's tune past the first minuet. Until now, I always respected the gel's intelligence, but love has clouded her mind. She cannot see that you will be unhappy if you have your way. And believe me, you idiotish man, your happiness is second only to Nan's where Jane is concerned."

He dared not trust his voice to respond, even if he had known what to say. He stared into the swirling brandy, its color so like the color of his eyes that he might as well have been looking into himself. But when he searched his soul for answers, he met a blank wall.

He could not seem to move beyond the wall to wherever Lady Swann was trying to lead him. Going there would shatter everything he had worked for. Without his goals, he had nothing. Without his dreams, he *was* nothing.

His eyes burned. *Love has clouded her mind.* He must have misunderstood. Damn, he had been witless since Lady Swann first went on the attack. If Jane Ryder cared for him, he had never detected any sign of it.

To be sure, there was the time he'd kissed her and felt an instant response, but most females responded when he kissed them. It occurred to him that he was confusing his own response with Jane's. Perhaps *he* was the one who had felt something out of the ordinary during those few precious moments.

Very well. Kissing her had rocked him on his heels.

But kisses meant nothing. He was a man. Men kissed willing women in hopes of more, and forgot them—the kisses *and* the women—soon after. That had always been his experience.

"Gone missing in the brain box, sir?" Eudora tapped her glass with her lorgnette to get his attention. "Well, never you mind. I've said what I came here to say. Ain't my way to meddle in another's business, y'know."

He shot her a scathing look. "You will understand that I find that hard to believe."

"Oh, quite. It's God's own truth, though. Although I am known, for reason, as The Tongue, I rarely interfere to such a degree as this. It gives me no pleasure to do so, even when I've a fondness for one of the gudgeons running amok. That would be Jane, of course. You, Fallon, are purely a disappointment to me on every count."

"I am devastated to hear it."

"You demmed well ought to be," she snapped. "I cannot decide which is the greater looby, you or Jane, the both of you convinced she's the one ain't good enough when it is clearly t'other way around. No use trying to convince her otherwise, though. *You're* the one must come to scratch, Fallon, not that I imagine for a moment that you will. You are too proud. You'd rather stay lost on a bad road than admit you took a wrong turn or were headed the wrong direction from the first."

Her words resonated with the unsettled feelings thrumming inside him. She made it impossible for him to dismiss them or force them from his mind as he'd been trying to do since bidding Jane Ryder farewell.

But the old busybody was wrong about what he thought of Jane. There could be no question of her worth. She was a finer person than he, by a long shot. He admired her enormously. Hell and damnation, he *wanted* her. His bed felt like a glacier at night with her not in it.

Even so, was Lady Swann actually suggesting that he *marry* Jane Ryder? That was patently impossible. Out of the question. Until she brought it up, the idea had never even occurred to him.

He recaptured his straying wits. "If it is her reputation that concerns you, Miss Ryder has assured me that she will in no way be sullied by our enforced . . . er, proximity at Wolvercote. Nothing of consequence happened between us, you may be certain."

"Oh, I can readily believe it. You have cat-lap for blood, and Jane will carry her virtue to the grave before romping with a man who fails to love her. Foolish gel. Had I been so nice in my ways, I'd have remained virgin until my third marriage. Or was it my fourth? Who can remember?"

She waved a bony hand. "I admit the obvious—a devoted man is in every way a better lover. But those are few and far between, and no woman of any sense waits very long for one to cross her path."

"I profoundly hope that Miss Ryder will do so," he said, trying not to imagine her in another man's arms. "She deserves better than a sordid back-corner affair."

"To be sure. But most folk never get what they deserve, for good or ill. 'Tis the way of the world." She emitted a gusty sigh. "The ones that do, go after it tooth and nail, never mind the consequences."

"Which is," he said stonily, "precisely what I am doing now."

"Cloth head! Let me tell you the plain truth, Fallon. You care only for the opinions of people you have yet to meet. You are attempting, with marginal success, to make yourself into what you think they expect of you. You have made yourself the slave of public opinion, which—trust me on this—is of less worth than a cup of warm spit."

"You speak nonsense," he fired back. "I mean to establish myself, and my family when I have one, where it belongs. Do you suppose I take pleasure in this tomb of a mansion, or the approval of strangers, or the prospect of courting a female simply because she has the breeding and the status to ensure our children their rightful place in Society? It is all for the children, Lady Swann. I shall never be fully accepted, nor do I care, but *they* will. And I'll do whatever it takes to make sure they are."

Her expression softened, but only for a moment. "Well said, m'lord. All balderdash, of course, but I take your point. What would the beau monde have to say should you wed the likes of Jane Ryder? My heavens. A bastard girl the next Marchioness of Fallon? It is too fearsome to contemplate. And since Jane will never let go of Nan, you would also be forced to welcome into your home the child of your father's bastard."

"Don't use that word! They could not help how they were born."

"No more than you," Lady Swann said gently. "But if you are enchained by preposterous notions of what you owe to the Fallon name, can you expect that Jane and Nan will not feel subjected to their own unfortunate heritage? Lord knows that Society would make them aware of it at every turn of the card, if they dared to show their faces among the very people you wish to join."

Fallon felt the ground melting beneath his feet. "I do what I must. I have sworn it."

"Only to yourself. Who else gives a groat what becomes of the Fallons? Tell you what, boy. Your father and grandfather and great-grandfather were scoundrels of the lowest order, but they had the bottom to do exactly as they pleased. Not a one shriveled up at the thought some high stickler might scratch him off her guest list, or that Lord Nobody would give him the cut direct."

"I concede you the point, madam. But the promises a man makes to himself are inviolable. In my own way, I have always tried to be honorable. And who can trust me, if I cannot trust myself?"

"Humbug! You have talked yourself into the very creature I feared you would become. Told Jane so, the very afternoon you first came to call. Fallon means to be a self-righteous, misguided, arrogant prig, I said." Lady Swann sagged back on her chair. "And I am so very sorry for it. This one time, I had hoped to be proven wrong."

Fallon felt heat stinging his cheeks. "I hardly think—"

"Of course you don't," she said brusquely. "Men have their uses, but thinking ain't one of 'em. And I am done beating my brains against a fence post. Ring for that flea-witted butler, will you, and have him summon a hackney. I also require a brace of healthy young bucks to cart me out of here. That freckled boy with the big shoulders is a good choice. I may hire him away from you."

Fallon crossed automatically to the bellpull, his mind flying off in a thousand directions. Damn her. After blasting him broadside with all cannons, she meant to sail away and leave him foundering. What the devil did she expect him to do? As the water closed over his head, he yanked the rope with a vengeance.

"I'll have my carriage brought around," he said with forced politeness. "There will be a short delay while the horses are attached. May I pour you some brandy?"

"Yes indeed." She held out her glass for a refill. "But make certain your servants move quickly. Jane must not know I have come here. She was gone to the shops when I stole away, and I must be snoozing in my parlor before she returns."

Fallon met Larch at the door and gave orders for the carriage and footmen. Then he returned to Lady Swann, only because it would be insufferably rude to leave her to wait alone.

She sipped at her brandy, ignoring his presence. Because she was altogether disgusted with him, he supposed. But then, he was pretty much disgusted with himself. He cast about for something to say.

"I would ask that you give my regards to Miss Ryder," he began awkwardly, "but I expect that is not possible. Under the circumstances. As you were not here, and have not spoken to me, you can scarcely convey a message. From me to her, that is."

"Oh, do stop rabbiting on, Fallon." She shook her head. "And have another drink. You're white as a sheet."

Because I'm drowning, he thought. *Soon to be fish food.*

"I am concerned for Miss Ryder," he said, blundering ever deeper with every word. "You have raised doubts in my mind. But they are, unless I am much mistaken, of no significance. By your own account, and hers, too, she will do better if we have no direct contact from here on out. And when she is wed, with children of her own, I am persuaded that she will scarce remember me at all."

Lady Swann only looked at him. After several moments, he began to grasp the nature of the evil eye.

Finally, to his relief, a pair of brawny footmen entered the drawing room, one of them the freckled youngster who had caught Lady Swann's fancy.

She immediately beckoned him closer. "What is your name, boy?"

"P-Peter Goodbody, ma'am." His face went scarlet when she rubbed her hand up his leg.

"Oh, my! Was ever a man so aptly named? Lord Fallon has said that you are to escort me home, Peter Goodbody." Her gaze lifted to Fallon. "Is that not correct?"

He waved approval, feeling rather sorry for the hapless young man. Jaw tight, he followed the small procession to the pavement and saw Lady Swann settled in his carriage, young Peter seated beside her. For a few moments, he stood with his hand on the open door. "Good-bye, Lady Swann. And please, do not fail to send the direction of your house in Bibury. My solicitors will contact Miss Ryder to make final arrangements for the settlement and allowances. I assure you, they will be generous."

"Yes, yes, the money will flow. I have no doubt of it. 'Tis a simple matter to dig into your pocket, after all." With that, she rapped on the panel and the coach immediately lurched away from the curb. A footman ran after and managed to close the door.

Feeling more stiff and lifeless than a tin soldier, Fallon made his way back to his study, sat behind his desk, and carefully sharpened his pen. He placed a fresh sheet of paper on the blotter, dipped the pen in the inkwell, and wondered what the deuce it was he had meant to write just before Lady Swann erupted into his well-ordered afternoon.

Richard Wellesley's invitation swam into his vision. Ah, yes, the Twelfth Night dinner, and the two young ladies Wellesley wished him to meet.

He was forced to make three attempts before producing a neat, unblotted acceptance. When a servant had been dispatched with the letter, he remembered to inform

Latmore of his plans and instruct him to lay out formal dress.

He wanted to make a good impression, after all. Tonight would mark the beginning of the rest of his life.

Chapter 16

All the guests invited to Lady Swann's Twelfth Night party were male.

The celebration had been Jane's idea, but since she had no friends of her own to invite, Eudora kindly agreed to act as hostess. Not that she ever considered doing otherwise, as Jane very well knew.

Enthroned on her Bath chair by her favorite spot near the hearth and, not by accident, directly under the kissing bough, Eudora was in exceptionally high spirits this evening. And in excellent looks, Jane had assured her truthfully. She wore a satin gown of vivid blue to match her eyes, and a paisley shawl of purple and carmine and teal. A brace of peacock feathers towered over her jet-black curls.

The parlor blazed with light. Jane had affixed red and green ribbons to the silver candelabra and hung wreaths of evergreen and holly on the walls. That very afternoon she had purchased a lovely crèche of carved cherrywood, complete with shepherds, angels, Magi, sheep, and a donkey. The Baby Jesus looked a trifle glum, and she rather wished for a goat to complete the scene, but it all fit nicely on the mantelpiece.

Eudora's antique servants would have been overwhelmed by thirteen seated to dinner, so Jane hired, over Cook's vociferous objections, an "assistant" chef and two serving maids. Lovely smells wafted up from the kitchen—eel soup, roast goose, baked salmon, mince pies. . . . Jane's mouth had been watering all afternoon.

Shortly before eight o'clock, when the guests were expected to begin arriving, Felicia toddled off to bed. Two helpings of rack punch had done her in, and old Mr. Mantooth must have dipped heartily, too. He was snoring in his chair by the front door when the knocker sounded.

Suspecting an explosion could not waken him, Jane decided to leave Mr. Mantooth where he was and opened the door to the first of Eudora's gentleman friends. To her astonishment, he was a young man, no more than thirty, with a round pleasant face and gentle brown eyes.

Smiling shyly, he removed his hat and bowed. "M-Mumblethorpe, ma'am, at your service. I expect you are Miss Ryder. Lady Swann has told me about you. Most pleased to make your acquaintance."

"And you are most welcome to come in, sir," she replied with a curtsy.

"I am early, I know, but my invitation instructed me to arrive betimes. Unless I am mistaken, Lady Swann has appointed me to act as her cicisbeo for the evening." He flushed to the roots of his receding hairline. "It is a great honor, to be sure, but I'm afraid I haven't the slightest notion what she expects me to do."

"Whatever she tells you," Jane advised, instantly drawn to the earnest, impeccably dressed gentleman. "She will not hesitate to make her wishes clear. Doubtless she will wish you to sit close by her, and I suggest that when you make your bow, you also take note of the mistletoe suspended above her head."

"Ah. Thank you, ma'am. It happens I am a bit near-sighted and was like to offend her from the very first."

Jane had scarcely led him to Eudora when the knocker sounded again, and for the next half hour she was kept busy ushering one elderly guest after another into the parlor. In all her life she had never received so many compliments as she did in that delightful thirty minutes. Each gentleman bowed with old-fashioned courtly grace, kissed her hand, and pronounced himself overwhelmed by her charms.

185

She had met them before, of course, when they called on Eudora, and they had always greeted her politely. But on those occasions she was merely a secretary, working at her desk while they cozed with Lady Swann. This night was altogether different. They had put on their party manners and approached her with the deference they might accord a duchess.

The Earl of Roedale arrived with several bottles of champagne, specially selected from his cellar for this splendid occasion. Lords Filbert and Doughty wore brightly colored brocade coats, even brighter waistcoats, and pearl-buckled high-heeled shoes. Powder from their tye-wigs dusted their shoulders and caused them to sneeze repeatedly into their lace handkerchiefs.

Sir Liston, who had limped in on a crutch, was sufficiently healthy to pinch her derriere when she leaned over to place a tapestry stool under his gouty foot.

She was half in love with them all by the time she could count eleven guests in the parlor. Like Eudora, they had refused to allow creaky joints and aching bones to diminish their hunger for life. While two maids circled the room with platters of hors d'oeuvres and cups of lethal punch, the men ate with relish, drank rather too deeply, and told decidedly improper stories. Jane hoped that supper would be ready before they were too foxed to locate the dining room.

She could not help but notice that Eudora kept glancing toward the parlor door as if expecting someone else to arrive. For that matter, she had ordered an extra place be set at table, insisting that thirteen for dinner was an unlucky number, although Jane had never known her to be the least bit superstitious.

How she would miss this extraordinary old woman! Eudora Swann was her dearest friend in the world. She had never loved anyone nearly so much, not even her mother, who always treated her well enough, considering that she blamed Jane for making the both of them social outcasts by being born. As if a babe had any choice in the matter.

Mortified to feel tears burning at her eyes, Jane slipped from the parlor and went to her bedchamber, where Nan was sleeping peacefully in her crib. Mrs. Gillis, the wet nurse, had already retired to her bed in the next room.

Jane disliked the woman, who made her living nursing one infant after the other with no apparent fondness for children at all. On the whole, the goat at Wolvercote possessed a better disposition than Mrs. Gillis. But she had agreed to come with them to Bibury and remain until a local woman could be found, so Jane was careful to keep on good terms with her.

After adjusting the blanket that Felicia had embroidered for Nan with her arthritic hands, Jane took a moment at the mirror to powder her nose and straighten her hair. She was wearing a gown of muted gold sarcenet, which had been folded up in tissue paper since she bought it on a whim several months ago. With the gold stars Eudora had given her shining on her earlobes, and the Kashmiri shawl that once belonged to Lord Fallon's grandmother draped around her shoulders, she felt positively elegant.

There would be no call for such finery in Bibury, she thought, or ever again. Only this once, at her Twelfth Night party, could she disguise herself as a gentlewoman.

Widgeon, she chided, heading downstairs to the kitchen where Cook was stuffing an apple into the open mouth of a roast suckling pig.

"We're all but ready to serve," Cook said, licking her fingers. "But the goose ain't quite crispy. Mebbe twenty minutes, Miss Jane."

"Thank you. But do tell the maids to stop dishing up the punch. And when they pour wine at supper, an inch in each glass will do. Otherwise, we are like to have eleven gentlemen sleeping under the table tonight."

"Wouldn't be the first time," Cook responded with a

wink. "In the old days, scarce a night went by without three or four cat-shot nobs snoozin' where they fell."

Laughing, Jane stopped by the dining room to make certain everything was in order. Eudora had put out the name cards herself, making sure each gentleman was placed near his friends. She would be seated at the head of the table, of course, with Jane at the foot and the empty fourteenth chair to Jane's right.

Then she noticed that someone had set a high-backed chair where Eudora's Bath chair would need to be. Crossing to the far end of the room, she pushed it against the wall. And while her back was turned, she heard the dining-room door open and close behind her.

She glanced over her shoulder.

Her heart made a flying leap to her throat.

Lord Fallon, spectacularly handsome in black evening dress, his collar and neckcloth snowy white over a silver-threaded waistcoat, gazed at her with an unreadable expression on his face.

Clutching at her shawl, she made a slow turn on watery legs, putting one hand on the edge of the table to steady herself.

Fallon's lips moved and tightened and moved again, as if he was trying to say something.

She summoned a polite greeting, but it never made its way past her constricted throat.

And then, with an oath, he charged across the room, knocking over a chair on his way, and pulled her into his arms. There was nothing gentle about his kiss. He held her as if fearful she would try to escape, and ravaged her mouth with lips and tongue while one hand threaded through her hair and the other clenched her around the waist.

She had never thought to see him again or be in his embrace once more. But here he was, his heart pounding against her breasts as he held her even closer. She thought she would die from the joy of it.

And then she thought she might really die if he didn't permit her to breathe very soon.

He lifted his head just as she began to push him away. She kept both hands open against his chest as he moved his own hands to her shoulders and gazed down at her, searching her face. He looked nearly as bewildered as she felt. It was a wonder they didn't melt together into a puddle on the floor.

"I should not . . ." he began slowly, his voice hoarse. "That is, I did not mean to . . ." He took a deep breath. "You see, Lady Swann said—"

"That you should kiss me?" Jane offered, trying to help. He looked so very angry with himself. She longed to smooth his harsh, frustrated expression and kiss the muscle ticking wildly in his cheek.

"No. Well, yes, if not in so many words. Dammit, Jane, I thought I'd worked out a proper speech, but now I can't seem to think." Color rose on his face. "Well, she did tell me that much."

"Eudora said that you cannot *think*?"

"Something to the effect, yes. She scrolled through a litany of my faults along the way, but that seemed to be the most significant. And she was right, of course, for I am everything she said and more. Above all the rest, I have been monumentally stupid. Which can come as no surprise to you, I warrant."

"I have never thought so, my lord."

He smiled faintly. "Now who is lying through her teeth? Confess it, Jane. You thought me a clodpole every time I behaved as one, which I've done on a regular basis since first we met."

Oh, no, she told him with her heart. *I thought you quite splendid. I still do. I always will.* But she could only gaze mutely into his eyes, unable to speak the words aloud.

"Well, then," he said, "I take your silence for consent. But I am glad of it. If Lady Swann was correct in her judgment of my character, she must know yours equally well. I can only hope, please God, that the rest of what

189

she told me was true. She came to see me this afternoon, you know. In a hackney cab."

Jane's heart settled somewhere between her toes. "To inform you that I have decided to remove to the country next week," she murmured. "She had promised me she would not, until after I was gone."

"I expect Lady Swann makes promises when they seem called for and keeps them when it suits her." His fingers tightened on her shoulders. "I had a right to know, Jane. Why did you feel a need to steal away from me?" He shook her gently. "There are limits even to my own monstrous stupidity. Be sure of this, my dear. Whatever happens now between us, I will never take Nan from you."

Relief washed over her. "Truly, I never believed you would. But I feared it all the same." She nibbled at her lower lip, wondering how to explain. "There was a big yellow barn cat where I lived once, and she was friendly enough unless she'd just littered kittens. Then, whenever I found where she was nesting, she would wait until I'd gone and move the kittens to another place. It was purely instinct for the cat, my lord, and much the same with me."

"I understand," he said quietly. "If you wish to go off to Bibury with Nan, then you must do so. Our agreement stands and I shall honor it in every way, including my promise to contact you only through my solicitors. Which I have just broken, to be sure, but I'll not do so again if you insist. Do you, Jane? Dare I beg you to change your mind?"

She stared at him, afraid to hope, knowing that what she hoped for could never be. "T-to what purpose?"

"Marriage." His gaze lifted to a spot over her head. "Lady Swann said that you are, unaccountably, in love with me. Is it true?"

She thought fleetingly of lying to him, for both their sakes, but could not bring herself to do it. "Yes," she said simply. "Yes."

Instantly she was enveloped in his arms again. "You will not be sorry," he whispered shakily. "I swear it."

"I know." How could she ever regret loving him? "But it changes nothing, my lord."

"The hell it doesn't!" He lifted her chin with a gloved finger. "You love me, but you don't want to marry me? Why the devil not?"

It was time to put space between them, she knew, reluctantly slipping from his arms and moving to the other side of the table. She looked back at him, across six feet or so of polished mahogany, resting her hands on the back of a chair for support. "You know the reasons very well, sir. I have told you who I am, what I am, and the Marquess of Fallon cannot—"

"Enough! If you mean to fling at me all my own nonsense about restoring the Fallon name to social prominence and wedding some twit because she comes with impeccable credentials and—God, I can scarcely bear to think on it." His voice softened. "That's all done with, Jane."

Only put aside for the moment, she knew, because he had discovered that someone loved him. She suspected that no one ever had, except possibly his grandmother. And he desired her, she knew. But desire was a long way from love, and even love could not bridge the chasm between them.

"You are an impetuous man," she began carefully. "You've a tendency to leap into action before considering what you are about, and you never think at all of the possible consequences."

He looked amused. "What you mean is, I charge in like a rhinoceros. But now and again, Jane, even a man blinded by his own preconceptions may stumble in the direction he ought to go. Or, in my case, be pushed there by a devious old woman."

"Lady Swann can be most convincing," Jane admitted. "But she is rarely practical, especially when it comes to matters of the heart. You have become caught up in one of her romantical plots, sir. You chanced to arrive on the scene when she no longer required a secretary and was casting about for something to do with me. I'm afraid that her affection for me has led her to forget who and what I am."

"Trust me, she has done nothing of the sort. But she put me in mind of who *I* am, just in time to prevent me from making myself into the even more repellent creature I was determined to become. The paragon of a marquess would have been a damnably unhappy man, Jane. I find myself unwilling to accept a dreary life for the sake of some fool notion an adolescent boy got into his head twenty years ago."

"It wasn't a fool notion," she protested. "It was your *dream.*"

"It was my nightmare. But I'm wide awake now. And if it matters, I relinquish nothing of any value whatever. This was always about family, about being ashamed of the one I came from and wanting to create a new one. And with little idea what a family ought to be, I aimed instead for what I could measure. Mind you, I still mean to restore Wolvercote and sire a generation of Fallons who will do credit to themselves. With you as their mother, they cannot fail." He held out his hands. "Come here, Jane."

She wrapped her arms around her waist to keep herself in one piece. One of them had to be strong, after all. But oh Lord, to bear his children! *Lead me not into temptation,* she prayed.

"Has that yellow barn cat got your tongue, Miss Jane-who-is-determined-to-protect-Lord-Fallon-from-himself Ryder? And need I remind you that patience is not among my questionable stock of virtues? I want you always to come to me freely, to be sure. But if you will not, be even *more* sure that I'll come after you. Must I jump this table?"

"L-Lord Fallon—"

"My name is Charles," he interrupted softly. "Can

you ... will you ... just for a moment, forget titles and obstacles and whatever else is stampeding through your beautiful head and listen? This is between Charles and Jane, my love. Only the two of us."

My love.

She might have rushed around the table, or perhaps she soared directly over it. But he was there to catch her, and suddenly she was in his arms, lost in another of his earth-shattering kisses.

"All will be well," he murmured when he finally lifted his head and brushed a tear from her cheek with his fingertip.

"I'm not usually such a watering pot," she said, sniffling as he wiped away another tear. *"Truly."*

Smiling, he located his handkerchief and put it into her hand. "I choose to believe those are tears of joy, my dear, but would rather Lady Swann not see them and conclude that I bullied you into marrying me."

To her own horror, Jane emitted a giggle. Good heavens, she really must pull herself together before he changed his mind about spending the rest of his life in company with such a widgeon. But she giggled again at the very idea of it. Plain Miss Ryder and the Marquess of Fallon. Who could have imagined such a thing?

Eudora. Bless her heart, Eudora had imagined it, and set the wheels in motion, and gone in person to browbeat Lord Fal—Charles—when her plot ran onto rocky ground. Thank God she was even more pigheaded than her stubborn protégés.

"I expect that Lady Swann is waiting for an *announcement*," she said. "Or does she know you are here at all? Have you been into the parlor?"

"Not yet. A young man let me into the house, and when I asked for you, a maid said that she'd seen you go into the dining room. I came directly here. But you may be sure that witch-woman knows we are together. Shall we go put her mind at rest?"

He stole one more kiss in the entrance hall before

opening the parlor door. It hit the opposite wall with a bang.

Laughter and conversation faded as he took her hand and led her into the room and past the gauntlet of curious eyes to the chair where Eudora sat proudly erect, a satisfied smile curling her lips.

Fallon bowed. "Your servant, Lady Swann. I am profoundly in your debt."

"So you are, rascal. When is the wedding to be?"

"Unless Jane wishes otherwise, as soon as I have procured a special license." He grinned. "Or have you already seen to that?"

"I might have done, had I been more certain the prospective groom would come to his senses. I'll give you one thing, Fallon. You have put me to more trouble than any man in memory, including all six of m'spouses, God rest 'em. I only regret failing to entice you to my bed. It's not too late, you know. I could teach you any number of ways to please your new wife."

Jane felt the roots of her hair go on fire from embarrassment as Charles dissolved in laughter.

"Ah, well," Eudora said with a heavy sigh. "Young men these days don't know what's good for them. I warrant every other man in this room would leap at the invitation." There was a sound of general agreement from the fascinated onlookers as she turned to Lord Mumblethorpe. "Have you the item I told you to fetch from the desk?"

Mumblethorpe located a thick stack of papers under his chair and placed it on her lap.

Jane recognized the nearly completed manuscript of *Scandalbroth*. She watched Eudora run her hand affectionately over the book they had worked on for more than a year and knew that she was saying good-bye. Then she beckoned to Fallon. Jane squeezed his hand before releasing it and stood aside.

"My wedding gift to you," Eudora said tartly. "This is the only copy, although I should warn you that Jane can reproduce it from memory if you give her cause. You may do with it what you will, of course, but I notice that the fire could use a good stirring."

Nodding, he took the manuscript from her lap and immediately consigned it to the flames.

"Well, that's that," she declared, raising her lorgnette to survey the rapt spectators. "Shall we go into the dining room, gentlemen? Mumblethorpe, you may push my chair."

The guests lined up in procession behind Lady Swann as Jane went to join her betrothed by the fireplace.

"Fallon, that's a kissing bough over your head," Eudora called from the doorway. "But don't be too long about it. We'll soon be toasting your happiness with Lord Roedale's excellent champagne."

Even before Sir Liston had limped from the room on his crutch, Jane was caught up in a pair of strong arms. At her back she felt a rush of heat as the fire consumed the last bits of *Scandalbroth* and turned the disreputable Fallon history into ashes. And then, lost in Charles's ardent kiss, she forgot the fire and the book and her own name.

When he finally released her, she was certain this man had no need whatever of Eudora's lessons in how to please a woman.

"Wonderful tradition," he said, pointing to the kissing bough. "I mean to have one of these permanently installed in every room at Wolvercote."

She brushed a vagrant lock of hair from his forehead. "I imagine the footmen and chambermaids will make very good use of them. Shall we join the others now, before Eudora comes scooting after us?"

"Not yet, love. First, I wish to call on Mistress Nan and see if she remembers me."

Jane led him to the bedchamber and used the single candle burning there to light an oil lamp while he dropped to one knee beside the cradle.

Nan lay sleeping on her back, hands curled alongside her ears. Her little bald head gleamed in the lamplight.

She must have tugged off her nightcap again, Jane thought, and played with it awhile before tossing it to the floor.

"How tiny she is," Charles whispered. "A breeze could lift her up and blow her away."

"You won't think so when you come to know her," Jane said, her heart pounding to see the unguarded affection on his face. "She is unmistakably a Fallon, I am persuaded—obstinate, impatient, and determined to have her own way."

"Excellent. We shall deal together famously." He grazed her plump cheek with his forefinger. "Won't we, Nan?"

At the touch, her eyes shot open. She looked first to the lamp Jane was holding over the cradle, trying to focus, and then to Jane, and finally to the dark-haired man leaning over her. Her mouth split in a toothless grin.

"Ga!" she pronounced. "Aga goo ga."

"A bit lacking in the conversational department," he said, grinning back at her. "How soon before she learns to talk, Jane?"

"Oh, months and months."

"Nonsense. This one will be jabbering away within a fortnight. May I pick her up?"

"Certainly. Don't forget to support her head."

He slipped one gloved hand behind her head and the other around her back, standing as he lifted her carefully and cradled her against his chest. "Hullo there," he said. "What a little beauty you are. Will you mind very much if I steal a kiss?"

Nan studied him intently for a moment. Then her right hand shot up and grappled his nose.

"Thee rememberth me," he said to Jane, looking excessively pleased.

"There can be no doubt," she assured him. "I have never seen her do that with anyone else, not even the wet nurse, and Mrs. Gillis has a nose the size of a cucumber."

Chuckling, he gazed with unconcealed love into the

infant's wide blue eyes. "Now pay attenthion, Nan, becauth thith ith import'nt. I am going to teath you your vewy firth word."

Jane wrapped her arm around his waist. "Good heavens, Charles. Do you want the child to grow up with a lisp?"

"Never you minthe her," he instructed the child. "Are you lithening?"

Nan smacked him on the cheek with her free hand. "Ga!"

"Ecthelenth. An' now, my prethiouth—can you thay *Papa*?"

On sale now!

In Regency England, there is a very thin line between
love and hate and betrayal . . .

ENTWINED
by Emma Jensen

Nathan Paget, Marquess of Oriel, returns to London society a great military hero of the Peninsular Campaign and a most eligible bachelor. Unbeknownst to the rest of the world, Nathan has been blinded and has only one goal in mind—to uncover the traitor responsible for the death of his comrades and for his injury. He shares his secret with only one person, the headstrong and beautiful Isobel MacLeod, who agrees to serve as his "eyes" and help him unmask the traitor in their midst. This unlikely duo can barely stand each other's company—or so they think until they find themselves falling deeply in love, a love threatened by an unknown enemy with murder and betrayal in his heart.

Published by Ballanntine Books.
Available in your local bookstore.

*Don't miss this enthralling new romance,
in a special keepsake hardcover edition!*

SOMEONE LIKE YOU
by *Elaine Coffman*

Reed Garrett is a down-on-his-luck cowboy who wanders Texas looking for work and a place to hang his hat. Then he finds himself on the doorstep of the willful and lovely Miss Susannah Dowell, a spinster who runs a small farm for her great-aunts. The last thing Susannah is looking for is a man, especially one as handsome and charming as Reed Garrett. But soon she begins to see beyond his sexy exterior to the complex wanderer harboring a heartbreaking secret from his past.

SOMEONE LIKE YOU is a wrenchingly romantic story of two lonely hearts who come together for a second chance at love and a first chance at real happiness.

Thrilling . . . heartrending . . . romantic . . .

**Now available in bookstores everywhere
from Fawcett Columbine.**

Romance Endures in Columbine Keeper Editions!